Leah

Leah

JAMES R. SHOTT

CARMEL • NEW YORK 10512

Library of Congress Cataloging-in-Publication Data
Shott, James R., 1925-
   Leah / James R. Shott.
      p.   cm.
   ISBN 0-8361-3526-1
   1. Leah (Biblical matriarch)—Fiction. 2. Bible. O.T.—History of
Biblical events—Fiction. I. Title.
PS3569.H598L4   1990
813'.54—dc20   90-35487
                                                                   CIP

This Guideposts edition is published by special arrangement
with Herald Press.

LEAH
Copyright © 1990 by Herald Press, Scottdale, Pa. 15683

Library of Congress Catalog Number: 90-35487
International Standard Book Number: 0-8361-3526-1
Printed in the United States of America
Design by Paula M. Johnson

To Mrs. Dorothy Ralston Crocker

Most people call her "Dorothy."
Seven people call her "Grandma."
Seven more call her "Great-grandma."
I am one of the privileged few
who can call her "Mother."

J.R.S.

Leah's eyes were weak,
but Rachel was beautiful and lovely.
—Genesis 29:17
(Revised Standard Version)

Leah had lovely eyes,
but Rachel was shapely and beautiful.
—Genesis 29:17
(Today's English Version)

1

Briefly but spectacularly the sunset flared, as though trying to make up in beauty what it sacrificed in time. Jacob watched, fascinated, as orange and red faded into the softer blues and purples of the desert night.

It was time for his bride to come to him.

After the feasting and revelry of the day were done, Jacob had gone to his tent, situated among palm fronds at the edge of his uncle Laban's oasis in Haran. He had made himself comfortable at the door of the tent to watch the sunset and await his bride.

He waited alone. According to custom, his family should wait with him, but he had no family. His father was dead. His mother was hundreds of miles away. His brother hated him. He was alone, but only for a few minutes. Then he would have a new family.

His wait wasn't as feverish and bride-hungry as he had expected it to be. The desert shepherding must have taught him patience. He had waited seven years for this moment. He could make it through an extra few minutes in the cool shadows of the evening. It was like being thirsty and looking at a cool flask of water for a moment before drinking. The anticipation added flavor to the realization.

Seven years! He had thought it long at the time, but now as he looked back, it seemed he had first laid eyes on Rachel just yesterday. Uncle Laban had rightly predicted the years would seem like days. Now that it was over, he found it pleasant to think back on.

During those seven years, he had done everything his future uncle and father-in-law had asked. He had tended sheep, learned about goats, supervised flocks, kept records. He had mastered all the small and large tasks involved in managing a successful sheep and goat enterprise. He knew the business now, even better than Laban's sons. He smiled smugly. Laban's flocks had grown in the past seven years, and he was at least partly responsible. He had introduced a few innovations, including an accounting method for breeding, a system he had learned from his father, Isaac. He was ready to become the full partner with Laban's sons that his marriage to Laban's daughter now entitled him to be.

And Rachel! Through seven years of seeing her occasionally at water holes, at sheep and goat pens, and in Laban's tent, his love for her had grown. He thought of her dimpled cheeks, her ready smile, her flashing eyes. In all that time, he had never seen more than her face. He could only guess at the athletic body hidden beneath her voluminous robes. Well, he'd explore her hidden grace soon enough.

Jacob noticed a small movement at Laban's tent, a hundred paces away. They were coming. The wedding procession began with Laban, solemnly leading the bride. Heavily veiled, she held her father's hand. The five sons followed. No other women were permitted in this wedding procession. It was men's business.

Slowly and deliberately they walked. Jacob was unruffled. He thought again of the flask of water in the hands of a thirsty man. He would savor the moment, anticipating that sweet sip at the end. Slowly getting to his feet, he calmly waited for them to arrive.

Laban stopped ten paces in front of Jacob. The wedding ritual was imminent.

"This is my daughter. I certify that she is a virgin."

Jacob said nothing. He could not accept his bride until she was formally handed over to him.

Laban continued. "I give her to you in marriage. You are now my son. May the *teraphim* of this house bless her womb, and give you many sons."

"Thank you, my father. I accept her as my bride."

Laban stepped forward, holding the heavily veiled woman's hand. Jacob stepped forward also. Laban solemnly placed her hand in Jacob's, bowed, and turned away. Then he and his sons marched off, crossing rapidly the hundred paces back to Laban's tent.

Without a word, Jacob led his wife inside. The tent was dark. He bent to light a lamp, but felt a hand on his shoulder. "Let it remain dark," she whispered.

Jacob's embrace was tender as he pressed his bride to him. He rejoiced as he felt her response. She gave herself to him freely, saying nothing, abandoning her body to his. The hours passed in blissful silence, at times with ecstatic frenzy, at times with soft rapture. Jacob marveled at the depth of the experience: a coupling of mind and body, a blending of the animal and the spiritual, a deep touching of souls. Drinking the flask of water was certainly more satisfying than contemplating it.

Eventually they drifted off to sleep in each other's arms, their bodies sated, their love enriched by their sensual passion—as though in sleep their souls were interlocked as securely as their bodies.

Jacob awoke as tendrils of sunlight crept tentatively into the tent. Drowsily he reached for the woman beside him. She lay on his forearm with her back to him. He stroked her thigh, slowly and with anticipation.

Coming out of his languid drowsiness, he wanted only to join himself with his beloved again.

Suddenly his hand stopped as he caressed her thigh. The flesh beneath him was smooth and exciting. But there was something wrong. He came fully awake and looked. The body was long and lanky. It had none of the athletic grace and smoothness he had imagined to fit the laughing face of Rachel.

He gasped. This was not Rachel! This was another body, a substitute, an impostor! Roughly he grasped her shoulder and turned her over.

Leah!

Rachel's older sister stared back, cowlike eyes opened wide. The receding chin trembled slightly, and her mouth opened to disclose uneven teeth.

Jacob sat up with a jerk. A cold feeling tingled his skin. He began to sweat in the crisp morning air. His sluggish mind at first confused by what he saw before him, he managed only to stammer, "Wh-where's Rachel?"

The big eyes before him filled, but she said nothing. He thought back over the blissful hours of the night, the impassioned coupling, their mutual love. "Was it you . . . I mean . . . last night? . . ."

She nodded. Her eyes, beneath the tears, were unbelievably expressive. The fear he saw in them was gone, replaced by sympathy and compassion. She actually felt sorry for him!

He caught his breath. A surge of rage replaced his bewilderment, erupted from his lips in a snarl, and exploded in a savage backhanded slap on her face. The blow was far more vicious and brutal than he had intended. She fell back on the carpet with a sob.

He raised his hand to hit her again, but abruptly his fury subsided. A drop of blood appeared on her lip, and bitter tears in her eyes. He felt a twinge of guilt.

He stood up. "We'll see about this," he muttered angrily. Jerkily he put on his robe and headpiece and pushed aside the tent flap. Custom demanded that he not leave the tent at all during the bridal week, but he was in no mood for such conventions.

The hundred paces to Laban's tent did nothing to cool his rising temper. By the time he got there, he trembled with rage and hurt. The fury erupted in a shout: "*Laban*!"

His uncle stepped quickly from his tent, fully dressed, his hair and beard combed and oiled, as though he were expecting Jacob.

"I am here, my son."

"Where's Rachel?"

"She's out in the pasture, with her sheep."

Jacob gaped at him. "Then . . . then . . . you knew! You—"

Laban remained composed. "Calm down, Jacob. I'll explain everything. But first, control yourself."

Jacob began to splutter some more, but in the face of Laban's composure, he subsided. Mastering himself with an effort, he forced his body to stand still. He glowered at his father-in-law, waiting for him to speak.

"Good. Now I'll explain."

Laban's urbanity was irritating. Jacob clenched his fists, feeling his nails bite into his hands.

Laban continued. "It isn't our custom to marry the younger daughter before the older. If we allowed that, Leah would probably never marry. So it was important that she marry first."

"But . . . you knew it wasn't Leah I wanted. It was Rachel. You cheated me!"

"You may have Rachel too, my boy. But you must accept Leah first."

"But I don't want Leah. I want Rachel!" The words sounded stupid, repetitious, even to Jacob.

"It's done now," said Laban, his voice soothing. "You've spent a night with Leah and consummated your marriage. You must give her the entire marriage week. Then you may have Rachel."

"But—"

"One week."

For a long moment, silence hung between them in the cool morning air. One week. Jacob turned it over in his mind. He recalled his passion, his conjugal bliss, with his bride last night. It was . . . bearable.

"All right," he said at last. "One week. I'll give her that. But only if I can have Rachel."

Laban nodded slowly. "Yes. Yes. Of course. But there is the small matter of the bride-price. The seven years you worked for me was to pay for Leah. Now you must give me another seven years for Rachel."

Jacob gasped. He could hardly believe what he had just heard. "But I gave you seven years. Why should I give you fourteen?"

"The seven years were for Leah. You owe me another seven for Rachel."

"But I've already waited seven years for Rachel! Must I wait seven more years for her?"

"No, my son." Laban smiled condescendingly. "You may marry her next week, immediately following your bridal week with Leah. When Rachel's wedding is over, then the seven years of service will begin."

When Jacob returned to his tent a few minutes later, he was filled with conflicting emotions. He was still hurt and angry at his father-in-law and disappointed and bitter that his new bride was not the one he loved. Yet he found it hard to resent Leah. It wasn't her fault. She was an unwilling lamb in her father's flock.

Leah waited for him in the tent, her body shrouded in the large shapeless burnoose she normally wore. Only her face was visible. Again he was aware of her eyes. So big! Yet, in a strange way . . . attractive! Something about them . . . something deep inside them. . . .

He frowned, pushing down the feeling of guilt as he saw the livid bruise on her swollen lip. He had every right to strike her. Yet the common custom of wife-beating had always repulsed him. Isaac had never laid a violent hand on his mother, Rebekah. But perhaps Isaac had never had just cause, as Jacob had.

Nevertheless, he wanted to be stern with her. He wanted to make her feel crushed and submissive. He wanted to stand before her as the injured husband who would graciously forgive her for the wrong she had done him.

"Leah."

"I am here, my husband."

What an absurd thing to say. She had been standing there before him since he had entered the tent, looking properly contrite and submissive. She moved her head slightly to hide the bruise on her lip.

"Leah, are you all right?"

She nodded. "It's nothing. I understand why you struck me. You're angry. You have every right."

As subdued as she was, he could afford to be solicitous. "It's not your fault, Leah. It was Laban's deception. He's to blame."

"You're mistaken."

The soft word filled the tent. Jacob looked at her, frowning.

"You should know the truth, Jacob. It was I who suggested to Father that we deceive you. The fault is entirely mine."

Jacob shook his head, bewildered. "You? But . . . why?"

"Because I love you, Jacob."

Those big eyes looked directly at him. They were filled with—with what? Understanding? Compassion? Sympathy? Or . . . love? Yes, love! That's what he read in those eyes!

He could read those eyes so easily. Her soul was bare before him. He could see all her secret thoughts and feelings just by looking into them. No wonder she was so honest with him. Those eyes would never let her lie successfully.

He struggled to maintain his anger and indignation, but they were beginning to evaporate in the face of this gentleness and beauty. Yes, beauty. He reluctantly admitted it to himself. Not the delicate animal beauty of Rachel; that was different. This was another kind of beauty, shown through those expressive eyes.

Laban had once called them "weak eyes." Weak eyes indeed! They were the strongest eyes he had ever seen!

It occurred to Jacob then that maybe his deal with Laban wasn't such a bad bargain after all. He would always love Rachel, but Leah wasn't entirely repulsive. She was certainly servile in her attitude toward him. He didn't think he could give himself to her again as he had last night, when he thought she was Rachel. But he could tolerate her.

Yes, and he would accept her love, even if he never fully returned it.

The next day, Jacob sat alone in a corner of the bridal tent. He sighed. This was only the second day. One day and two nights behind him . . . but five more days! Five interminable days until he would be finished with Leah and could have Rachel. The solitary desert pastures that had taught him patience during the past seven years could not prepare him for this.

Last night—their marriage week's second night—and yesterday had embarrassed both him and Leah. Last night, in spite of his good intentions, he had muted her eager response by his mechanical approach to lovemaking. He felt guilty, knowing of her love for him. And yet, he told himself, it was her own fault. She had baked her own bread. Now she must eat it.

He recalled the first night, with its wild rapture, its frantic efforts to draw closer to each other through connubial bliss, its tender moments of sensitive serenity, and its fusion of body and soul. What a contrast to last night! Last night had been spiritless, phlegmatic, dutiful. She must be aware of the contrast too, and hurt by it. Again, the stab of guilt.

As unpleasant as the thoughts of last night were, they were nothing compared to the memory of the long day yesterday. Once the initial shock had worn off, and the confrontation was over, Jacob had settled into a brooding, self-pitying silence. Sensing his anger, Leah had stayed out of his way. She had busied herself whispering with her new maid, Zilpah, whom Laban had given her as a wedding gift.

Five more days of this! Bridal custom demanded that he spend the entire week in the tent, getting acquainted with his bride. How ironic. The nights were for getting to know her body, and the days her mind. One week of close confinement with each other was supposed to seal the marriage, to bond them together for life. A wise custom, normally—but not when you're cooped up with the wrong woman!

How nice it would be to leave the tent, go off into the lonely desert with a drove of sheep, and savor the solitude of a long companionless day.

Somewhere out there was Rachel. Sooner or later he would find her at some secluded oasis. But it was out of the question. If he wanted to marry Rachel, he must stay here. He must remain in this tent, with the black sky of the tent ceiling a few feet over his head, a cow-eyed wife mooning over him, and a frightened maid servant darting furtive glances his way. Maddening!

The long stretches of solitude in the desert with his sheep had taught him how to fill the lonely hours, however. And he had learned that falling into moodiness was the worst thing he could do. It was so easy to slide into the dark hole of depression, to soak luxuriously in the sweetness of the ebony mood which tried to envelop him. It had happened to him before.

To counter it, he had learned in the wilderness to think bright thoughts, sing, talk to the sheep, tell them jokes, laugh and dance. He wished he could play a musical instrument like some of the shepherds. That was the best way to stave off madness.

Shaking off his lethargy, he looked around. He would have to do something. The dark mood had begun to grip him yesterday. He knew he must fight it today. He must try to talk to his wife. He hesitated, wondering if this dull-eyed woman could talk about anything cheerful or meaningful. But there was no one else to talk to except the new maid, Zilpah, and she seemed even more stupid than Leah. He had no choice. To fight the paralyzing depression, he must talk to his wife.

"Leah."

"I'm here, my husband."

"Sit beside me."

She felt for the carpet on which he was sitting and awkwardly sank down on its far corner. She didn't wear her headpiece inside the tent, and he noticed that her hair, although combed and oiled, was straight and stringy, a dull-colored brown. But he forgot her hair as he looked into those expression-filled eyes.

"Leah, tell me about your eyes. How long have they been weak? Did you injure them at some time?"

"I was born with weak eyes," she said softly. "They have always been this way."

"How much are you able to see?"

"Very little. I can see things I hold in my hand, although they're a little blurred. I can't see well what's on the ground when I stand up. If there's a stone, I can't tell if it's flat—or big enough to trip me."

He thought of the limited world in which she lived every day. "It must be hard for you, to be so handicapped."

"I'm used to it." The big eyes were now communicating gratitude for his thoughtfulness in this conversation. "It's true I can't go anywhere unless I'm walking beside someone who will be my eyes, but I've found much to compensate for it within my tent."

Jacob recalled then something that Laban had told him: Leah had taken over the management of the household after her mother's death. She had done a good job of it, in spite of her handicap.

He needed to say something comforting. "Then you don't really mind not being out in the pasture with the sheep, as Rachel is—"

The hurt in her eyes at the mention of Rachel's name stopped him. Was there rivalry between these two sisters? Perhaps there was another, less obvious, reason why they weren't close. Was she jealous of Rachel's eyesight, of Rachel's natural grace and beauty?

"Your eyes," he said softly. "They're beautiful, in their own way. They're so expressive, so tender, like a . . . a. . . . "

"Wild cow," she said. "That's how I got my name."

It suddenly occurred to Jacob what she meant. The word for "wild cow" in their language sprang from the same root as the name "Leah." He didn't know if love or derision lay behind her naming. If derision, it was cruel. He hadn't known Leah's mother, who died before Jacob came to Haran. But he did know it was the custom in that country for the mother to name the children.

Jacob said, "Would you like to know how I got *my* name?"

"Oh, yes!" Leah's eyes sparkled. She really did want to know; he could see it in those remarkable eyes.

"Jacob means 'grasping.' My mother named me at birth. I'm a twin. My brother was born first, but I came out from my mother's womb immediately afterward, grasping his heel."

She smiled shyly at this, and he was drawn to her eyes again. When she smiled, it seemed her eyes smiled, too. He could see in them a childish delight, as though she were pleased he was sharing himself with her.

"Were you a shepherd before you came here?" she asked.

"My father and grandfather were shepherds before me. And, of course, I've been keeping sheep for years. This experience with your father's goats is new to me, though. I don't like goats as well as sheep."

"But goats copulate more readily than sheep," she said. "So they reproduce faster. They're hardier, resist disease much better than sheep, and their milk is a source of food. There are advantages in sheep, also. If you have both, they complement each other. They—"
She stopped suddenly and lowered her eyes.

"How do you know so much?" Jacob asked. He tried

to keep the tone of his voice friendly, not wanting to discourage her sharing.

"I listen." She glanced quickly at him, and her eyes said, *I'm sorry; I've been talking more than a wife should.* "I've heard men talking about it in my father's tent, and I . . . well . . . I listened."

She's not as stupid as she looks, thought Jacob. He remembered that she had used the word "copulate" when speaking of goats. This was a word men didn't use in the presence of women. It was something men *did* to women, not something they talked about with them.

He recalled another discussion he had had with Laban. So now he asked Leah, "What do you think about your people's practice of putting up solid-colored poles, so the sheep and goats will breed only solid-colored offspring?"

His question was presumptuous. He wasn't sure why he asked it. She could hardly know anything about such matters. Maybe that was why he had asked it. He found himself wondering if he were trying to put this girl in her place and assert his own masculine superiority.

Her answer surprised him. "A meaningless superstition. It has proven to be nonsense time and time again. Yet men will believe their stupid superstitions, and—" She stopped abruptly, lowered her eyes, and folded her hands in her lap. "I'm sorry. I have no right to talk like this."

Jacob was surprised that his feeling of irritation at her was not for what she said, but for her apology. He had been planning to squelch her, to put her in her place emphatically. Then she had done it herself. He decided to encourage her to talk.

"Please go on. You make much more sense to me

right now than even Laban does. What do you think about the solid-colored animals being stronger than the ringed and dappled ones? Do they bring the owner good luck?"

"More nonsense." The big eyes opened wide and came alive. "There's no relationship between skin color and strength. That's a superstitious tradition in Haran, passed from one generation to another. The older the tradition, the more easily it's believed. But it has never been true. I've always wondered why they continue to hold such foolish beliefs."

She's right about that, Jacob confessed to himself ruefully. His father had never said anything about it. There were many off-color sheep in Isaac's flock. They were as healthy and produced as many offspring of the pure white ones. She knew what she was talking about. But he didn't want to make this concession out loud. Not to her—a mere woman.

It was time to squelch her. To step on her as though she were a tiny bug, not an equal.

"Why do you suppose they follow that tradition in this area?" he asked innocently. He was digging a pit for her, and she rushed headlong into it.

"It's tied in with the religious beliefs of our country. We have the teraphim, our family of household gods which govern our family and fortunes. If we put up solid-colored poles, the superstition will work. If we don't, it will fail. The teraphim make it work or fail. If the god of our family is stronger than the god of another family, our sheep and goats will breed stronger and better offspring. So will the servants and wives. That's the common belief."

"But you don't believe it." Jacob's response was not a question, but an observation. He found it incredible that she would go this far. She not only talked authoritatively—like a man—on the breeding of animals. She addressed even religious matters confidently!

This bordered on heresy, challenging her family beliefs. Surely she would back off now. Nobody—especially a handicapped, stay-at-home, unattractive young woman—should hold such strong opinions. It wasn't proper. She was thinking and talking like a man.

"Of course I don't believe it." No backing off here. Her assertion took her even further into forbidden male territory. Jacob wondered if she were speaking thoughts she had never voiced to anyone before. Surely Laban wouldn't countenance such behavior in his daughter.

But she wasn't finished. "That's pure superstitious nonsense," she continued, her voice vibrant with enthusiasm. "Those gods have no power. The teraphim are supposed to be a symbol. But they don't symbolize anything. There is no family of gods, no power of any kind in those pieces of wood or the stupid gods they symbolize."

Jacob stared at her. The magnitude of her statement appalled him. Not what she said. He agreed with her. But the mere fact that she would say it.

The time had come to end this.

"This is heresy," he said sternly. "You never said anything like this to your father. He would beat you soundly for it, or even put you to death. I have the same right. Why are you telling me this?"

His voice was harsher than he had intended. The big eyes opened wide as they stared at him for a second. He could read in them not fear but hurt. Then she lowered them, bowed her head, and assumed her former attitude of submissiveness.

"I . . . I'm sorry, my husband. I have no right. But I thought. . . . "

"You thought what? That you have the right to share heresy with your husband? That you could presume to teach me something about religion?"

"Please forgive me, my husband." The big eyes opened. Again he could see no fear, only hurt and shyness. At least there were no tears. He didn't want to have to deal with that.

Her voice was soft. "I spoke to you this way because I know what you believe, Jacob. You believe in one God, the God of your grandfather, Abraham. You believe this God is the only true God, and that there are no other gods."

Jacob gaped at her. "How . . . how do you know that?"

"I listen." She dropped her eyes again and lowered her head, reminding him of someone in the attitude of prayer. "I've listened often to your conversation with my father. I . . . know a good bit about you."

He should be angry. He tried to be. But he wasn't sure what he felt. These past few hours of conversation had introduced him to a completely new person. Now he didn't know her at all.

"And what do *you* think of my God?" His question surprised even him. He found he really wanted to know.

Leah turned her eyes on him again, and he saw warm love for him shining in them. "It's good to believe in that kind of God," she said softly. "A God who acts like a God instead of a jealous household idol. Your God loves people and helps them rather than merely demanding sacrifices from them. Your God seems to be a God who would watch over individuals yet still allow them to seek their own destiny. You could pray to this God, and find meaning in the prayer."

The words were spoken slowly and meekly but passionately. Jacob could hardly believe what he had just heard. Here was a religious viewpoint that was mature, well thought out, springing from a sensitive and highly intelligent soul. He had completely forgotten his former resentment. He stared at her.

"You sound like you believe in this God."

"I would like to, Jacob. That's the only kind of God I would feel comfortable with. Please tell me more about your God."

"There's not much more I can tell you. You seem to know a lot already."

"Have you ever . . . had any—I mean . . . has God ever spoken to you? Or appeared before you in a shape you could see? Or is it just something you believe in your mind?"

"Our God doesn't usually work like that. God has no physical body to show people."

"Surely you must have had some kind of encounter, some feeling that this God was present. . . . "

"Well, I had a dream once."

"Tell me about it."

"It happened just before I came to your country, very shortly after I left home. I was traveling alone. That night I leaned against a smooth stone to rest. I was depressed and lonely. My father was dead. My brother hated me. I might never see my mother again. When I fell asleep, I began to dream."

Jacob paused, remembering. He had never spoken of his dream before. "Usually I don't remember my dreams. But this one was so vivid I can't forget it."

"Describe it to me."

"There was a ladder, a kind of stairway, stretching upward into the sky. It was surrounded by a bright glow. Then on the stairway I saw people, beautiful people, climbing up and down. And at the top. . . . " His voice trailed away.

"At the top? What did you see?"

"God."

"God? How can that be? You said you couldn't see God because God has no body to show people. How could you possibly see God?"

"I don't know. I don't remember exactly what I saw up there, at the top of the stairs. I feel sure, however, that it was God."

Leah nodded thoughtfully. "Dreams confuse me. Does God speak through them? Or do we speak to ourselves through them? Of course, even if you were speaking to yourself through your dream, you were touching your longing to see and believe in your God."

Jacob nodded. "But there's more. God said something. God told me who God was: the God of my father and grandfather. And God said something about the land."

"The land? You mean the land far to the west, where your family lives?"

"Yes. It's called the land of Canaan. The voice at the top of the stairway said it belongs to me now, and to my descendants. There will be many of us. And there was something else."

"Tell me."

"We will be a blessing to others. Through our family, the whole world will be blessed. What does it mean, Leah? Was God really speaking to me?"

"I don't know." Leah's thoughtful round eyes turned to Jacob with sympathy and understanding. "But the dream sounds like God's voice. And it certainly says something about you. You want—you need—a God who will be close to you. You want more than just a faceless God whom you believe in only with your

24

mind. You need a God you can meet face-to-face."

"Is my God such a God, Leah? Was that what God was trying to tell me in that dream?"

"I don't know, Jacob. I hope so. Perhaps someday you'll find out. Maybe we both will."

In that tender moment Jacob became aware of the serving girl, Zilpah. She was fussing around the edge of their carpet, working with the evening meal. Jacob's thoughts were wrenched back to the present. The evening meal! What had happened to the day? The long, boring day he had expected had flown by.

He looked at Leah thoughtfully. Before his gaze, she lowered her head and sat motionless. Who was this woman? A stranger sat on the carpet in front of him. He had known her body intimately during the night. Still she was a stranger. She might look stupid and cowlike, but she wasn't. Her eyesight was limited, but she saw so much! She could discuss the flocks and herds, their breeding and pasturing, with insight surpassing Laban's. She had a sensitive, mature approach to religion, and a deep understanding of his own yearning for God. Who was this stranger sitting here?

Under his penetrating gaze, she squirmed a little. Then she lifted her eyes and smiled shyly. There was nothing arrogant about her. How could he have believed her to be smug and supercilious, pushing herself forward where she had no right to be? She wasn't like that at all. Though modest and unpretentious, she had a good mind and a sensitive soul. This was probably the first time in her life she had an opportunity to express herself freely.

He would be talking to her all day again tomorrow. He looked forward to the next day, and more stimulating conversation with this strange wife. He wanted to get to know her better, to uncover more of her intelligence and sensitivity. And the days would pass quickly after all.

And tonight? Well, perhaps he could show a little more enthusiasm tonight, too. Perhaps he could find words to tell her, in the midst of their lovemaking, how much he appreciated her. It would please her. It took so little to please her. She had accepted the fact that he didn't love her, but it would be cruel now to pretend he felt nothing for her.

He wasn't sure what he did feel. Respect? Gratitude that his wife was more than a stupid sightless animal? Curiosity to learn more about this stranger? He didn't know. At least it wouldn't be boredom—either during the day or, hopefully, during the night.

It might be interesting tonight, he thought. And in spite of himself, he was looking forward to it.

2

The sun shone warmly on Leah's face. This was the best time of day. It was good to sit just outside the doorflap of the tent in the early morning. It was good to be warmed by the sun after the chill of the desert night. Soon she would seek the shadows inside the tent, but for a time she could enjoy the freshness of the morning.

The last day of Rachel's bridal week had finally come, and it had seemed eternally long. Leah had been married to Jacob now for two weeks. The first week had been filled with new discoveries: the joy of conjugal love, the pleasant hours spent talking with Jacob. But the second week was almost unbearable.

When Leah's bridal week was over, she moved to a nearby tent. She was grateful for that. She could never share her tent with her sister—not now. It was hard enough being in another tent, knowing that, just over there. . . .

The other tent was only a few paces away, although she couldn't see it. But she knew it was there. She could hear them. Their laughter. Their giggles. Even their moans. She had tried not to listen, but her hearing was more sensitive than most people's, because her ears compensated for what her eyes couldn't do. And so she had been sentenced to listen, listen to the al-

27

most deafening sounds of pleasure from the other tent.

Her mind went back to her own bridal week with Jacob. Only on the first night had she known the depth of love and ecstasy that Rachel must now have every night. And that was only because Jacob thought she was Rachel.

The other nights were pleasant but not completely satisfying. Jacob had been attentive and sensitive. He had tried his best to show a little enthusiasm beyond the dutiful role of husband. But it wasn't the same. Without love, sex became mechanical. It became an animal activity designed to bring about children, much like what happened in the flocks.

The daylight hours of the bridal week had been much better. Never had she been able to talk with anyone as she had with Jacob that week. All her life, like water wanting to overflow a dam, she had been filled with the need to talk with someone. With Jacob she could finally overflow, without fear or hesitation. Not even when he struck her after discovering her deception had she feared him. She knew Jacob. There was nothing to fear.

Leah bit her lip. She had talked too much. The dam had burst and poured out unchecked. Jacob probably considered her a long-winded shrew, like some of the old women in the marketplace. She smiled. She would try not to let the dam burst again.

But it was good to have someone to talk with, someone who understood, who listened without being offended.

Except he *was* offended. Several times. She had pricked his male ego when she told him her ideas about breeding and pasturing the herds and flocks, ideas even ahead of his own. She must be careful not to go too far. Perhaps a subtle suggestion, an unassuming hint, might lead him to believe it was his idea, not hers, for improving the animals. She mustn't forget she was the wife and he the master.

She wondered what it was like between Jacob and Rachel. Not physically; she didn't want to think about that. But their conversations . . . were they as sparkling and stimulating as hers had been? Probably not. Rachel had always been superficial and childlike. Never had she thought seriously about her life, or challenged time-honored traditions. Always cheerful and friendly, she would make a marvelous lighthearted companion for her husband. But she was far from his intellectual equal. Jacob probably enjoyed his days with her, but in a far different way from his first bridal week.

Now it was over. Last night had been the seventh. The bridal week was completed. Jacob would be leaving Rachel's tent this morning, and there was a good chance he would come over to Leah's tent to speak with her. She looked forward to this meeting, because she had exciting news to share.

Something—or someone—was stirring over there. Leah heard the rustle of the tent flap, then the crunch of sandals on hard ground. He was coming.

"Greetings to my first wife," said the familiar voice. "Are you enjoying the morning?"

"Ah. It is my first husband," she replied, smiling. "Come closer, so I may see you."

Jacob squatted on the carpet just outside the tent. She could see him now, but not clearly. She did see well enough to know that he was dressed to go to the fields.

"Are you going to the sheep pens today, Jacob?"

"Both Rachel and I are going for the day. We'll be back tonight."

Leah felt the familiar jab of jealousy. Quickly she

thrust it aside. At the same time she lowered her eyes, knowing they could give away her inner thoughts.

When she looked up, she smiled. "Then I'll have your evening meal prepared and waiting—for you and all your household." This, of course, would include Rachel and her new maid, Bilhah.

Jacob nodded. "You're very thoughtful. I'm grateful."

He was being formal. Perhaps he was eager to get on with his day's work and spend more time in Rachel's company. She must tell him now.

"I have something to tell you, Jacob. I hope it will be good news for you."

"I'm listening."

"I think I'm with child."

Jacob gasped. "Really? But how could that be?" It's too soon—" The words broke off in midsentence, perhaps in embarrassment. As much as he knew about the breeding of sheep and goats, he was lost when it came to the breeding of women.

"Perhaps it's too soon to know for sure just now. But I'll be certain by tomorrow. I'll tell you then."

He started to say something but fell silent. Leah thought she knew what he wanted but was too embarrassed to say. He wanted to know how she knew. But he didn't want her to tell him. It would mean talking about things men and women didn't talk about. Not even husband and wife.

She longed to tell him. They could discuss the gestation period of sheep and goats. But they couldn't talk of her monthly confinement. That was "unclean," as the men put it.

Women were just as bad, however; they delicately referred to it as "the time of the women." Yesterday her "unclean time" should have started, and she was regular. Never in her life had she been more than a day late. She was reasonably certain of her pregnancy now, but she told him to check with her tomorrow because she wanted to see him again. How sad, she thought, that she had to resort to subterfuges just to speak with him for a few minutes.

"Are you all right?" Jacob's face was serious now. She smiled at his innocence. "Is there anything I can do for you?"

"There is, Jacob." She laughed softly. "Just don't treat me as though I'm sick. I'm quite well. I'll be all right until my lying-in time comes."

"God be praised." It was a formula, but Jacob sounded as though he meant it. "I will have a son."

"Or a daughter."

"No. It won't be a daughter. God will give me a son. What will you name him?"

She breathed a sigh of relief. He obviously accepted the tradition of her people that the mother would name the child. Maybe because it was the custom in his land also. After all, his mother had come from Haran.

Leah had an answer ready: "Reuben."

"Reuben? It means, 'Behold, a son.' A common enough name. Why call him that?"

"Because I want you to see your son, Jacob. I want you to see him and be pleased you have a son." *And love me for it*, she thought but didn't say.

"I'll be pleased, Leah. You shall have my gratitude."

Leah dropped her eyes, hoping he wouldn't see their hurt. *It's not your gratitude I want.*

Jacob rose. "I must go to the field now. But what you have told me this morning has made me very happy."

"God go with you, Jacob."

"And with you, Leah."

Sandals crunched on hard ground as he returned to Rachel's tent.

31

The sun shone warm on her face. Too warm. Her sensitive skin prickled. Quickly she rose and entered the cool darkness of the tent.

She smiled as she recalled their parting benediction. So formal! "God be with you." But spoken so easily and naturally between them!

Only a month ago she might have said, "The teraphim go with you." But she wouldn't have meant it. At least this farewell had a ring of sincerity to it.

She stroked her stomach. It might still be a girl, in spite of their discussion. She smiled. She would ask Jacob's God for a boy. The first of many. May Jacob's God—no, *our* God—open her womb to many more. That way, perhaps Jacob would love her.

Reuben. "Behold, a son." She had chosen the name carefully, but not for the reason she had given her husband. She had told Jacob he would behold his son. But the name really meant that God had beheld *her*, God had looked at *her*, and given her a son. Because of that, her husband would love her.

3

Inside the tent, Leah sat on the carpet kneading dough for baking later in the day. She welcomed this dim and cool retreat. It gave her a chance to think about her family and the ten years that had passed since her marriage to Jacob.

Although the tent was dark compared to the bright glare outside now in the middle of *aviv*, the dry season, she was satisfied to remain indoors. More than most people, she felt at home in the nebulous world of the tent. The sunlight often burned her sensitive skin. It made Rachel's skin more attractive. . . . But she checked that line of thinking. The disciplined habit of many years automatically asserted itself. Her mind wouldn't let her edge toward jealousy of her sister.

She smiled, thinking about Jacob's God. She knew so little about God. Yet God had been good to her. In these ten years she had had six sons, four from her own womb and two from her maid, Zilpah. She called to mind a picture of each one.

Reuben. "Behold, a son" was as kind and thoughtful as a nine-year-old boy can be.

Simeon. Just turned eight, he had been named "He heard." Leah nodded. The first two children were named for seeing and hearing. Jacob's God not only saw her but heard her silent prayer.

And Levi. He was six and named "Attachment." She had never told anyone why she named him that. With three children, Jacob was now firmly attached to his unattractive wife.

The fourth child, Judah, was only five. Even at this young age, he had gone with the others to the field to tend sheep. A responsible boy. Well named: "Praise God!" She had told her husband that this signified her formal acceptance of Jacob's God. But secretly she knew it meant that God had blessed her with strong ties to Jacob, and she praised God for it.

All four boys were in the field with Jacob now. Each one, at the age of five or six, had left the tent to begin his training as a shepherd under his father's tutelage. She missed them, but they were well cared for, not only by Jacob but by Laban and all the others. The boys were well liked, especially Reuben, who had early endeared himself to everyone by his mature thoughtfulness and kindness.

Her last two boys were still in the tent. Another year would pass before Gad would go to the field, followed a year later by Asher. Their names held no special significance: "Good fortune" and "Happiness."

They were Leah's children, even though they had been born from her maid Zilpah's womb. Jacob had placed both boys on Leah's knees at birth, signifying that they were Leah's, and worth the same as the other four boys. Zilpah had accepted this without question. Her dull mind was satisfied with the ancient tradition that a wife's handmaiden becomes the husband's concubine and all children born to her become the children of her mistress.

Leah then called to mind the other two children now in the field with Jacob: Dan and Naphtali. They were Rachel's children through her maid Bilhah. In spite of the nights of lovemaking Jacob had spent with her, Rachel had no children from her own womb. She rightfully claimed the children of Bilhah as her own, but her jealousy wasn't as contained as Leah's. Her children were named "Justice" and "Struggle." Rachel never tried to hide her feelings about her sister's fruitfulness and her own barrenness. She even saw it as a contest between her household teraphim and Jacob's God, whom Leah had quietly accepted.

"My god has finally given me 'Justice,' " she had said when Jacob placed Dan on her knees.

Later, following Naphtali's birth, she had told Leah, "See, my gods are winning the 'Struggle' between us." But Leah knew that in spite of her claims of victory, Rachel was secretly hurt and angry because she had not given birth to children of her own.

Leah's thoughts of her family were interrupted by the swishing noise of the tent flap being pushed back. Someone was here. Not Zilpah; she had not had time to go to the spring for water. Was it Rachel?

"Hello, Mother!"

Reuben. She recognized his cheerful greeting. But what was he doing here in the middle of the day? Was there a problem in the pasture?

As Reuben came into her blurred field of vision, she saw he was carrying something. Still wondering about trouble in the pasture, she asked, "What's wrong?"

"Nothing, Mother. I've brought you a gift." Reuben laid what he carried on the carpet before her.

"Mandrakes." Leah picked one up and held the plumlike fruit in her hand. How like Reuben. Only trouble would bring most people to her tent in the middle of the day; with Reuben, it was to bring a gift.

"You're very thoughtful." Just how thoughtful, she well knew. Mandrakes were believed to have magical qualities; they were able to make a woman fruitful if she ate them. It was foolish, of course. A superstition. And Reuben knew it.

"May you have many more children," said Reuben.

Leah could see only the vague shadow of his face, but she knew he was grinning. This was a joke they could share between them.

But—it was more than a joke. Leah nodded. Reuben knew the hurt in her heart, the hurt caused by the end of Jacob's night visits. Until a year ago, his custom was to visit her tent several nights a month. But after Judah was born, Leah couldn't conceive again. Jacob, believing she was finished having children, spent no more nights with her. It hurt. It hurt deeply, because it showed why he had spent those other nights with her.

Leah herself had given up having more children. But she longed to spend another night with Jacob, to feel the warm tenderness in his embrace, to share herself with him in that unique conjugal union which is the deepest form of communication between man and woman. But her nights had been as barren as her womb, and it hurt.

Reuben knew, however. His gift was given not merely to cheer her up, but to delicately express his understanding. And he was only nine.

"Leah." Rachel's voice. She spoke from the door of the tent.

"Come in, sister."

Rachel sat on the corner of the carpet beside Reuben. They were blurred outlines to Leah, but she knew exactly what passed between them. Rachel flashed him her dimpled smile, and he grinned. He loved his aunt Rachel; everybody did. She was so friendly and pretty. She was kind to everyone. Leah lowered her eyes and fought the old familiar battle within.

"I saw you coming in with the mandrakes," said Rachel. "Where did you find them?"

"In the east pasture near the oasis with the five palms. They grow wild there."

Rachel nodded. "I remember the place, but *I've* never seen mandrakes there before." Rachel's friendly voice seemed to say to Reuben, *you are more observant than I.* It was a subtle compliment, and Reuben responded with a warm smile.

"Leah." Rachel turned her smile on Leah. She couldn't see it, but she knew her sister, and she felt it. All her sunny personality, in fact, was in her voice. "May I . . . have them? Please?"

Leah hoped Rachel's eyes hadn't yet adjusted enough to the contrasting darkness of the tent to read what Leah's eyes reflected. But Reuben was studying her thoughtfully.

"Mother," he said gravely, although Leah recognized the amusement in his voice. "Why don't you give them to her? Perhaps they will be what she needs."

Leah quickly lowered her eyes, lest Rachel read in them the secret laughter she shared with her son. She didn't want her sister to think she was mocking her.

"Thank you, Reuben," she said. "But I won't *give* them to her. I'll *trade* them."

The friendliness in Rachel's voice changed to guarded suspicion. "Trade them? For what?"

"For one night with Jacob."

Rachel laughed. Leah knew why. There was no threat here. Leah was just love-hungry. Rachel would gladly trade one night of love for the secret leading to conception. She would do anything to conceive; this was a small price. And without the mandrakes, Leah would not conceive again anyway. Or so Rachel thought.

"All right then," Rachel said. Then turning to Reuben she said, laughter dancing in her voice, "And what are you grinning at? You're too young to understand."

Leah smiled. He understood more than Rachel realized.

Reuben stood. "I'll return to the field immediately. I'll find Jacob and tell him he's needed at Leah's tent. Then I'll keep my brothers in the field tonight. You'll not be disturbed."

"Thank you, Reuben."

His thoughtfulness amazed her. Their desert tent had little privacy. It was bad enough to share the tent with a maid and two small boys. They had all grown accustomed to the sounds of lovemaking. They had to—being alone was impossible. But when boys approaching puberty were in the tent, it was different. That was embarrassing, and the lovemaking became self-conscious and somehow vulgar.

Late that afternoon, Leah was led by four-year-old Gad to the edge of the spring, just a hundred paces from her tent. There she would wait for Jacob.

She didn't have long to wait. She heard Jacob's familiar step near the spring where she had been waiting less than an hour. As Jacob greeted her, she could hear his concern.

"How did you get here?" he asked. "You shouldn't wander so far from the tent."

"Gad brought me here. He wanted to know if he could go to the field yet. That's the fifth time he's asked me this month. And he still has a year to go."

"Impatient boy! He's more like Zilpah than you."

Leah's hand clutched Jacob's sleeve, and together they walked slowly toward the tent.

"Reuben said I was needed in your tent," said Jacob. "Is anything wrong?"

"Nothing wrong, Jacob." Leah tried to keep her

voice lighthearted. She hoped her eyes reflected good cheer and humor. "I've just bought and paid for you."

"Bought and paid for me? Am I a sheep that I can be bartered in a business transaction?"

Leah laughed, recognizing the amusement in his voice. "I bought you for the price of those mandrakes Reuben brought in from the field today. I traded them to Rachel in exchange for spending the night and the next day with you in my tent." The "next day" hadn't been part of the bargain, but Rachel and Reuben would never know.

Jacob's hearty laughter spoke more than his words. He didn't resent being bargained over. On the contrary, he enjoyed it. It subtly flattered him, and he willingly entered into the spirit of the game.

"So that's why Reuben kept the other boys in the field for the night! He's sly, that one!" The word was "sly" but the meaning was "thoughtful." Jacob was as proud of his oldest son as Leah was.

"I know why you want me in your tent tonight. That's easy enough to understand. But why tomorrow also?"

They had reached the door of the tent, and Jacob stooped to enter first. A proper wife never walked ahead of her husband.

"That will wait until tomorrow," Leah replied. "Let's take one thing at a time."

How could she tell him that a day with Jacob meant as much to her as a night? It wouldn't be so if all the nights could be as that very first night. But that wasn't to be. His love belonged to Rachel, and Leah had to content herself with a dutiful joining of bodies as he gave her what was her right as a wife. It was pleasant but not perfect.

And so day was as enjoyable as a night. The coupling of two intelligent minds in stimulating conversation and planning was almost equal to the joining of two bodies. Those times of conversation together had increased as they grew older. They discussed many things: the flocks and herds, the children, the family problems, even religion. They could share each other in this way, and enjoy it as much as sexual union.

The smell of mutton stew pervaded the tent. Jacob and Leah sat together on the carpet while Zilpah served them. Leah had long ago dismissed the tradition that men and boys would eat together, then the women and girls could have anything left over. While that tradition prevailed in Rachel's tent, it didn't apply here. Jacob had accepted this. An intimate dinner with Leah wasn't unpleasant to him.

"Tell me what you want of me tomorrow."

"I've said before, Jacob, that will wait for tomorrow. We shall take one thing at a time."

"Well . . . all right. What else can I do? I've been bought and paid for, like a ram. And so I shall act the part. Tonight, you'll wish you were a ewe instead of a woman!"

Leah's laughter at this didn't reflect her true thoughts. If only it weren't so! How often she *had* felt like a ewe with her ram when she was with him at night! *Rachel* felt like a woman. Abruptly she turned aside her thoughts in that direction. This was her night with Jacob. She mustn't spoil it.

4

Leah lifted her face into the light morning breeze, savoring its refreshing embrace. She dipped into the quiet pool by the spring to wash her face. The warm sun on her face was invigorating. A month had passed since the *malkosh*—the last rain of the wet season—and the lambing had been completed two weeks ago. This was *aviv*, when the barley ripened and the gardens were ready for harvesting. It was good to be alone and savor the delicious feel of morning.

She had come to the spring alone this morning for the first time in her life. There was nothing to fear, she told herself. Even if she got lost and wandered out into the desert, someone in the oasis would soon be up and see her. But she wanted to be alone with her thoughts for a few minutes, before everyone in the tent woke up.

She smiled; it had been a satisfying night. Her mind drifted back over Jacob's tenderness, his passion, the strength of his encircling arms. If only she had his love, like Rachel had night after night—but she must squelch such thoughts.

This day would be even better than the night. She reminded herself to be cheerful rather than gloomy, humble rather than self-assertive, to do more listening than talking. Jacob must not be bored, or he would go back out to the field by noon. He never observed the rest period in the middle of the day and wouldn't hesitate to go back to the sheep if the day turned tedious. That mustn't happen. She wanted him for the whole day.

She recalled another promise she had made to herself: she wouldn't let him think she was trying to run his business for him. She wouldn't tell him what to do or insist he do things her way. Like most men, Jacob was easily offended when a woman asserted herself. His masculine ego demanded he take the lead, whether in love or business matters.

Business matters. That was what she wanted to talk about with him today. Her mind was seething with ideas, plans, hopes. She frowned. If only she could find ways to lead his thinking with small hints, encouraging him when he followed up on her suggestions. They must end up as his ideas, even though she had spent many hours thinking them through. But she must be careful. If he thought they were her ideas, he might reject them.

She heard the crunch of his sandals even before he spoke her name.

"Good morning, Jacob. May God give you a pleasant day today."

But he was in no mood for pleasant formalities. "Leah, how did you get here? You never came this far by yourself. What if you had missed the spring and wandered off into the desert?"

"Then," she said, trying to keep her voice light and cheerful, "I suppose you would come after me, and drive me back to the tent like a wild cow."

She breathed a little easier when she heard him laugh. "And I would drive you back with a stout stick, you may be sure."

The moment was precious, warmed by the fresh sunshine and cooled by the crisp morning air. She hoped to remember it always. He squatted beside her at the pool.

"And now you must tell me why you bought and paid for me today."

She smiled shyly at him. "Conversation. I want to talk with my husband. I get lonely sometimes, alone in the tent all day. I need something to do . . . someone to talk to."

This wasn't exactly true. There were plenty of people to talk to: Rachel, the maids, the children. There were many little tasks to be done, and she was constantly busy. Would Jacob understand? Would he sense her loneliness, her reaching out to him, her need to share the intimacies of her mind with someone her equal?

For a brief moment, he sat silently, staring at her. At last he sighed. "You're more than a ewe who needs a ram to satisfy her. Well . . . all right. Where shall we begin? I suppose you want to know all about the new lambs, and those goats that were sick, and how the barley harvest is progressing."

She breathed a sigh of relief. He understood. At least, she hoped he understood.

"Tell me about the lambs first," she said. "How many? And are they healthy?"

"Our last count was fifty-two new lambs. The last two died shortly after birth. They were weak anyway, and their mothers should never have been bred in the first place. The lambs born in the middle of the wet season are the strongest. They're doing well."

"What are their colors?"

"Thirty-two are white. We separated the other twenty immediately. You know how Laban feels about black sheep, or even those that have a spot of color on them.

He has them slaughtered before they're old enough to breed."

"I know. He thinks they're weak and bring him bad luck." This was an old topic of conversation. She must move on before Jacob became bored.

"It's a shame so many good animals have to be killed," she said. "Couldn't you persuade Laban to keep them?"

"Do you think he would? You know your father!"

"Maybe . . . maybe he would give them to you."

"Why should he do that?"

She shrugged. "A gift, maybe. A token of appreciation for your faithfulness during these years. Surely he owes you something."

"I've already received my wages for fourteen of those years. You're half of them."

"But the fourteen years have become seventeen years, Jacob. What about these past three years?"

Jacob was silent a moment. When he spoke, his voice was soft, pensive. "I've been thinking about asking him for wages. Of course, if I stay with him till he dies, I'll get a share of the inheritance. With your five brothers, my share will be one-sixth."

"Is that what you want? To stay with my father until his death, and then inherit one-sixth of his estate?"

"No." Again Jacob paused before continuing. "That's not what I want," he said finally. "I really want to be in business for myself. If I ask for wages, such as a few sheep and goats for each year's service, maybe I can begin to build my own herd."

"But—would my father give you anything? I'm sure he wouldn't want you to grow as wealthy as he is."

"You're probably right. He wouldn't give me even one good ram or ewe for breeding, unless—"

"Unless what, Jacob?" Leah held her breath, willing

44

him to answer with the idea she had been working on for the past few weeks.

"Unless he gives me the weak ones, the off-color ones. He would gladly give them to me, and laugh at me behind my back for my foolishness."

"And how would you feel about your . . . er, foolishness?"

"My 'foolishness' would probably build up to a sizable number of black sheep and spotted goats. He wouldn't laugh at me long once he saw my success."

"You know so much about breeding. You could build up a full flock in two years."

"You're right!" Jacob's enthusiasm was unmistakable. "I wouldn't want to interbreed them; that weakens them. I would begin with the twenty lambs Laban rejected this season. And the goats—there are twelve of them now waiting to be slaughtered. They have white markings on them. It would be easy to breed them with some of Laban's animals that have been known to produce off-color offspring. I would choose only the strongest ones for the breeding—"

"But would Laban let you interbreed with his animals? Especially the healthy ones?"

"Probably not." Jacob frowned as he thought about this. "In fact, he would probably do whatever he could to keep his strong rams from my spotted ones."

"But what if you bred them before spotted poles?"

Leah's question was asked innocently, and she quickly lowered her eyes, lest he read in them her deception. She had been thinking about this for days. But it had to be his idea.

Jacob's quick mind immediately grasped the sense of her suggestion. "Of course! Laban would permit his strong rams to breed before *spotted* poles!" He laughed without humor. "After all, a solid-white sheep that mates before a spotted pole could never produce a healthy offspring!"

He rubbed his hands enthusiastically. There seemed to be no resentment that the suggestion had been hers, not his. It would be just like him to believe it was his idea in the first place. She hoped that would be the case.

The sun had climbed into the sky, and the fresh cool air was turning hot on her skin. She pulled the hood of the burnoose around her head to protect her face from the sun. Jacob noticed and was immediately solicitous.

"It's time to go back to the tent," he said. "You mustn't stay out long in this heat."

At least he was kind enough not to add what he was undoubtedly thinking—that Leah couldn't take the sun like Rachel, who went day after day in the heat without apparent harm. In fact, it only made Rachel more beautiful. But he said nothing, and Leah was aware that over the years he had learned to respect her sensitivity and didn't compare his two wives. At least not out loud.

In the cool shadows of the tent, Jacob squatted on the carpet opposite Leah. She watched his vague outline as he sat calmly and seemingly at ease, but she sensed that his active mind was whirling with ideas and plans.

"I'll put up the spotted poles at certain oases," he said, his voice vibrant. "Then I'll carefully select which sheep and goats I'll bring together. There will be no indiscriminate breeding. There shall be two qualifications for those I bring together: they must be strong, healthy animals, and they must have a history of producing off-color offspring."

"But what if my father and brothers become suspicious of your methods, and won't allow their animals to be bred before the spotted poles?"

"At first, they won't suspect anything. But after a year or so, when he sees my success in breeding off-color animals, he'll tell me not to breed any of my animals with his. He'll probably try to keep our flocks and herds separated. But by that time, it will be too late. I can have a large and growing nucleus of off-color sheep and goats."

"But won't he be suspicious about the spotted poles? You know he believes in that old superstition. Won't he think the spotted poles are the cause of your success?"

"Of course he will; that's the point. It may be several years before he realizes the poles have nothing to do with it—if he ever does. In fact, I'll let him change the poles on me if he wants. That will keep him busy, while I go on with my breeding. He'll try to devise ways to outwit me—all involved with those silly poles."

They talked on through the lazy afternoon. Jacob talked about which goats and which sheep would be mated, and how he would divide the flocks and herds to do this. Occasionally Leah offered a suggestion, but her attentive encouragement kept him talking almost incessantly.

"I'll go see Laban tomorrow," Jacob said. "I'll demand my wages. Surely he can't refuse me this simple request."

"But won't he be suspicious if he sees you so enthusiastic?" Leah asked. "He may not know what you're going to do, but he'll wonder why you're so eager to have all the off-color animals."

"You're right. How can I broach the subject to him so he won't suspect?"

"Why don't you tell him you need your wages because you want to go home?"

47

Jacob frowned. "I can't go home, and Laban knows it. I've told him about my brother. He'd never believe me."

"Maybe he will, if you tell him you want to know if your mother is still living, and to see your father's grave. You could say you're homesick for the sight of the hills after being so long in flat country."

"All that is true," said Jacob. "I *have* wanted to go home for years. The only reason I haven't is because of my brother."

"Speak of this to Laban. He might believe you. And if he does, he'll do anything to get you to stay. Especially if you point out to him how much you've done for him, how the flocks and herds have increased under your management. You might even say your God has blessed your efforts—"

"Which is true."

"And my father would accept that. He's so gullible in anything that touches religion. He somehow thinks your God brings you good luck."

"If that's so," said Jacob, "won't he also think my God will increase my own herds and flocks, even if they're off-color?"

"He might, Jacob. But would he care? After all, they're the weak ones. And if they're bred before spotted poles, what difference does it make to him? That's how he'll think."

"You're probably right."

"And one more thing." Leah paused. Slow down, she told herself. You're talking too much. He might think they're your ideas, not his. But—she had to say one more thing.

"There is greed. My father likes being rich. He never has enough. That's why he'll believe what he wants to believe."

"And," said Jacob, the words tumbling out, "he'll think he's putting one over on me. Again. He's done it before, when he gave me the wrong wife, and now he thinks—" Jacob caught his breath.

"Forgive me, Leah. I shouldn't have said that."

"It's . . . all right, Jacob. I understand."

It must have been her eyes again. She couldn't keep anything from him. Why must they show so clearly the pain in her heart? And why should there be any pain at all in her heart today? After last night's pleasure, and today's sharing, she should be content. But still the old wound hurt.

He had given her much in the past seventeen years. He had given her a home, security, tenderness. He had shared his body and his mind with her. Yet the only thing she truly wanted he could give only to Rachel.

Abruptly she pulled the curtain down on forbidden thoughts. She struggled back to the present, aware of Jacob's concerned gaze.

"I understand, Jacob. Let's not allow old wounds to scar the last moments of a pleasant day."

Jacob's relief at her attempt to spare him her feelings was evident in his voice. "And was it a pleasant day?"

"It was. A pleasant day and a pleasant night. It was well worth the price of a few mandrakes."

The reminder of the little joke between them brought a chuckle to Jacob's lips. "As though you needed mandrakes, anyway. Your fertile womb has brought me four sons now. And maybe—after last night —there will another one."

Leah frowned. Jacob didn't believe that, and neither did she. She had stopped having children. But she mustn't be bitter about it. Not now, when she had so much. And now she must try to keep up the jocular tone of their conversation.

"And if I do have another son," she said with a smile, "I'll have to think of another name."

"You already named six sons," said Jacob. "You should be running out of names by now. Tell me. What would you call him?"

"I think I would call him Issachar."

"Issachar?" Jacob burst into a hearty laugh. "Of course! 'Wages!' The perfect name. For you have bought and paid for me with a few mandrakes!"

If only it could be, thought Leah, as they laughed away the rest of the afternoon. If only she could buy her husband's love. But, she realized with a start, that's what she had been trying to do all along. Not with mandrakes, but with children.

She wished fervently that she could have another child. Then the word "wages" would find a new and secret meaning: another part of the wages she was paying for her husband's love.

5

___

To both Leah's surprise and Jacob's delight, the impossible happened: Leah became pregnant. When the child was born, it was a boy. How easily Leah gave him children!

Just moments after the birth, Leah sat upright on her bed and Jacob placed his son on her knees.

"His name is Issachar," she said.

"Leah," he said, his voice reflecting his pride. "We have nine sons!"

Leah smiled and held the little boy to her breast. He began to suck noisily.

"God is good," she murmured.

Jacob leaned back on his heels as he squatted beside Leah's bed. The scene was familiar. Leah knew Jacob had always enjoyed watching one of his sons draw life from his wife's breast.

"Nine sons." He rubbed his long black beard, running his fingers through the well-oiled hairs. "Nine sons. We'll have no problem when we're old."

Leah nodded. "I can well understand your father's fear when Rebekah had no children for so long. How he must have prayed for a son—and then God gave him two!"

"Yes," he murmured. "And one deserted his mother."

There was no mistaking the bitterness in his voice.

"But Jacob, Esau is there. He's taking care of your mother."

Jacob nodded, frowning. "That may have saved my life. I suppose the reason Esau didn't follow me here to kill me was because he had to stay home to take care of Mother."

"Then that means she's still alive. Do you think he still plans to carry out his vow? Maybe he has matured and outgrown his childish vengeance."

Jacob snorted. "Esau isn't the kind to change his mind. And besides, he swore a sacred oath. That can't be broken lightly."

"If that's so, what's to keep him from coming here after your mother dies?"

Jacob was silent. Then he spoke slowly. "I've been thinking about that for many years. I'm not sure what I would do."

"But Esau wouldn't dare harm you here. After all, you're under Laban's protection."

"I know. And I have nine sons who will soon be grown men. We should be well protected."

"But you're still not sure."

Jacob shook his head. "If you knew Esau. . . . "

"I think I know him well, from your description of him. He's fierce and ruthless. If he could, he would kill us all. But he's also honorable. He won't desert his mother. And he respects the laws of hospitality and won't harm you while you're a guest in his uncle's house."

Jacob stared at her. "You see things so clearly."

Leah cuddled the baby, who seemed to be giving her strength even as he drew strength from her. "But there's one thing more, which you must never forget."

"What is that, Leah?"

"God is with you. Remember, you're the heir to the Promise."

Jacob sighed. "I forget that sometimes. We seem so far away, here in Haran. Do you think God stayed back there in Canaan—with Esau?"

"No, Jacob. Don't ever think that. Look at what God has done for you during these past few years!"

That was certainly true. The success with which Jacob had built his own flocks and herds during the past two years had been phenomenal. Following this year's lambing, there were many more sheep and goats with color blemishes than there were solid colors. One more year, two at most, and Jacob's wealth would surpass Laban's. When Laban died and his estate was divided among his five sons and one son-in-law, Jacob would be the wealthiest man in the entire land of Haran.

"You're right, Leah," said Jacob gently. "You're always right. I feel better now. I won't forget again I'm the birthright son, the heir of the Promise. Thank you."

"God is good," murmured Leah. And she meant it. Jacob's God was as much hers as her husband's now.

Leah was glad Rachel's and her monthly cycles had never become identical, as they so often did with women who lived close together. This allowed Jacob to resume his monthly visits to Leah's tent during those times Rachel was "unclean." Perhaps he believed she could give him even more sons. She did. Another child was born to Leah, whom she named Zebulon. Very appropriately, his name meant "Good Gifts."

Then Leah, clearly not as far past her childbearing days as she had once believed, became pregnant again. Jacob had ten sons now, six from Leah's womb. So far, all his children had been boys. But Leah knew the hurt deep inside him, the hurt that not one of his ten sons had been borne by Rachel.

When Leah's baby was born, it was a girl. She named her Dinah. The name had no special significance, and Jacob took it as a sign from God that Leah's productivity was finished.

And then one day Rachel announced she was pregnant. Her face was radiant, and her dimples prominent. Jacob too was ecstatic. He told Leah over and over that God had finally opened Rachel's womb. May she have many more! If Rachel began to produce, Leah would no longer need to give him sons. He could quit those monthly visits to Leah's tent. He thought his words would relieve her. How little he understood!

When Rachel's time came, there was great rejoicing in the cluster of tents which made up Jacob's household. But the joy soon turned to fear. Rachel's labor was hard. For two days and nights, while Leah, Zilpah, and Bilhah attended her, Rachel screamed. Gradually her screams weakened. Jacob, though not permitted inside, kept an agonized vigil just outside the tent.

Shortly after noon on the third day, Leah came out of Rachel's tent and called to her husband.

"You have another son, Jacob!"

He ran to her and clutched her hands. "And Rachel? How is she?"

"She's very weak. But she'll be all right after a few days. Meanwhile, I'll nurse the baby with my own, until she gets her strength back."

"May I see her now?"

"Only for a moment. She's too weak. Please don't place the baby on her knees now. She can't hold him."

Leah stood just inside the tent door as Jacob knelt beside his wife's bed. Bilhah stood nearby, holding the newborn baby.

"Rachel," he whispered. "How do you feel?"

"All . . . right."

"I'll come back later, my love. When you're feeling stronger. I'll place the child on your knees then."

"No." Rachel gasped. She gathered strength for another word. "On my knees *now!*"

"But you're weak. Perhaps tomorrow—"

"*Now.*"

The voice was weak. The word was strong. Jacob took the baby from Bilhah and held him gingerly on Rachel's knees. Ordinarily she would be sitting up for this ceremony and would hold the child herself. But she lay supine and motionless, and he had to hold the child himself, just barely touching her knees.

Jacob seemed in a hurry to get the ceremony finished so his wife could rest. "What shall this child's name be?" he asked.

The word came from Rachel's lips in a whisper: "Joseph."

Leah caught her breath. Joseph meant "Another." The only obvious explanation for it was that she wanted another son. It seemed incredible, after what she had been through.

Jacob's voice was soothing. "Joseph it shall be. Now go to sleep. Everything will be all right."

He handed the child back to Bilhah and rose. Then with a nervous sigh he left the tent.

Leah followed him out. "Walk with me, Jacob." She had something to tell him. Something important. "Take me to the spring."

"It will rain soon. We can't be long."

"But it's important."

"I know." Jacob took her arm and led her. "You want to talk about the baby's name."

"Yes, Jacob. I'm not at all surprised. She wants 'Another,' and many more. Her need to have children outweighs the suffering of childbirth."

55

"But why?"

"Don't you know? She's in a contest with me. She has your love, and I have your children. Now she has your child. She wants more."

"I always knew about your rivalry. But I thought it was unimportant, like a joke between you. Does she take it seriously? Do you?"

Leah knew she couldn't lie to him, so she ignored the question. "With her," she said slowly, "it's a religious contest."

"What?"

"It's a contest between our God and the family teraphim. So far, God has proved stronger, for I've given you many sons. Now the teraphim are showing some strength. Did you know she wanted the two idols of the teraphim to be in her tent at the time of childbirth, one on each side of her during her labor?"

Jacob snorted. "What good would that do?"

"None at all. You know that and I know it. But Rachel firmly believes it. The only reason they weren't there was because our father refused her. In fact, he was angry that she even asked."

"But he has never refused her the gods before. I've seen them in her tent many times. Sometimes she even puts them beside her bed when we—sleep."

She dropped her glance when he said this. But he paid no attention to her hurt.

"Leah, you said Laban was angry that Rachel asked for the teraphim for the childbirth. Has he ever been angry with Rachel before?"

"Yes. And me also. In the past year, especially, we've noticed it."

"I'm not surprised." They had reached the spring and squatted down on the grass. This was a familiar spot. Often they came here to talk. The family and servants all respected their privacy and let them alone.

Leah looked up at Jacob. "You've noticed, haven't you, that Father has changed?"

Jacob nodded. "Yes. And your brothers have become openly belligerent. Just last week one of them challenged Reuben's drove of sheep at the north oasis. If it hadn't been Reuben, there might have been a fight. But Reuben backed off. And then, several times your brothers haven't waited for our flocks before opening the east well and dipping out the water. They've never been like this before."

Leah sighed. "They're jealous. Your wealth is like a slap in their faces. Like Rachel, Laban thinks there's a contest between your God and his teraphim."

"What should we do, Leah?"

There had been a time when Jacob would have been too proud to ask her advice. But he had changed over the years. It seemed natural for him now to turn to her as an equal and seek counsel.

"I think the time has come," she said slowly, "to move."

"Move?"

"Before there's bloodshed."

"But where would we go?"

"To the land of Canaan. Your old home. You've always wanted to go back. Maybe this is the time."

"But my brother—"

"I know. We've talked about that before. Maybe he no longer has that streak of violence."

"And his oath?"

Leah shrugged. "Well, that may be. But we can't stay here. Who do you want to face, my father and brothers, or your brother?"

"I don't think your father would kill us all. Esau might."

"No." Leah spoke the words calmly, feeling a deep assurance. "No harm will come to the heir to the Promise."

The sky had darkened; very soon rain would fall. Leah could smell it in the air. Jacob took her arm and slowly they walked toward their tents.

"We'll go." Once his mind was made up, he would forge eagerly ahead with his plans. "We can leave in two weeks, when Laban and his sons are occupied with the sheep shearing. We can slip away unnoticed, and it will be three days before Laban will even know we've gone."

"But your own sheep? They'll need to be sheared first. They can't go on a long journey in their heavy wool."

"We'll have to do it early. I'll tell our sons to begin immediately. That will at least keep us away from the oases where they might meet Laban's sons."

Jacob began to walk faster, either from the excitement of making plans to go home or because the rain was coming. Leah felt a drop on her head.

"There's a lot to do, Jacob. I'll see that everything is ready in our household. You take care of things in the field. And we'll need several camels." The camels would carry the women and small children.

This reminded Jacob of something else. "And Rachel? Will she be able to leave in two weeks?"

"She will. She's strong and healthy. A few days' rest is all she needs. But maybe you'd better explain to her about our leaving. She would accept it better from you than from me."

Rachel couldn't bear to leave her teraphim behind. But she would have to. She would have to obey her husband.

When they reached the tent, the rain began to fall.

58

The baby was crying inside. It was her hunger cry. But Jacob wouldn't recognize that.

"There's a baby crying inside your tent," he said with a smile. "A female baby. I know a boy's cry when I hear it. I'll not come in."

"You don't come in much anymore, Jacob. Just because she's a girl."

"You know my preference is boys. Sons. What good are girls? But then, when Dinah grows up, we can find her a suitable husband. Then she'll be worth something."

Cruel words, thought Leah, as Jacob left her tent and went toward Rachel's. He felt more at home there. Even though Rachel was resting, there was a little boy in that tent.

But he felt comfortable there not just because of the boy. Because of Rachel. His love for her—stifling the thought, she found solace in the sucking baby. Their little girl. Their only girl. Their last child.

There was sadness mixed with joy in that thought.

6

Jacob designated the western oasis as the place his clan should gather to depart from Haran. It had the largest water hole. They couldn't stay there long, however; so many flocks and camels and asses and cattle would strain even that water hole.

Leah had directed the household's preparations. Rachel was well enough to travel, gaining strength each day. There were two small babies to carry. Leah would carry Dinah herself, and Bilhah and Rachel would take turns carrying Joseph. The two boys, Issachar and Zebulon, though only two and three years old, would ride on one camel. It would be great fun.

Leah wished she could see the western oasis. She had never been here before, but she knew it was large. She asked Zilpah to describe the scene. Many sheep, many goats, many—whatever they're called—Zilpah couldn't begin to estimate the number. Leah had a general idea, however, and she pictured the scene in her mind. Hundreds. Stretching from one end of the oasis to the other. The moo's and baa's and hisses and shouts blended into a cacophony of organized confusion, adding to Zilpah's confusion.

"Black sheep. White goats. Spots. Rings. Streaks." Zilpah threw up her hands. "We'll all be dead before long!"

Leah laughed. Zilpah, of course, accepted the popular lore of Haran, that off-color animals meant weakness and bad luck.

Jacob himself was the last to arrive, with the camels. He came to his wives immediately. His first concern was with Rachel's health. He was relieved to find her strong and cheerful. Then he turned to Leah.

"We must leave as soon as possible. Laban suspects nothing; he's too busy shearing his sheep. My guess is we'll have three days before he discovers we're gone. Do you think he'll try to follow?"

"No." Leah's answer was firm. "Not after three days. It's not worth it to him. He wouldn't make a long journey just to say good-bye to his daughters. In fact, I think he'll be relieved we're gone."

"But won't he think we've stolen everything from him? Isn't it the custom of your people to believe that everything—flocks and herds and even daughters and grandchildren—belong to the patriarch of the clan?"

"That's true, Jacob, but I doubt he'll want to recover all those off-color animals. He's glad to be rid of them. And you—and your God. Now his teraphim can work unhindered."

"I hope you're right, Leah." Jacob shook his head and muttered something about it being time to get moving. He helped Leah mount her camel and told one of his sons to lead it. Then he helped Rachel mount and handed the baby Joseph up to her.

"If you feel weak or faint at any time," he said to Rachel, "be sure to call Bilhah to take the baby. I don't want anything bad to happen to our son."

Leah didn't miss Rachel's triumphant tone as she repeated Jacob's phrase, "our son." It was inevitable, she told herself. Joseph—the youngest—would be the favorite.

The journey was long, arduous, and uneventful. After a week, Jacob quit worrying about pursuit. He confided in Leah that he was glad to see hills again. He had been in the desert too long.

Each night they camped in a place which could be easily defended in case of attack. Jacob was careful to post guards around the camp. He instructed them each night to be vigilant. But there was no trouble.

They arrived in the hill country of Gilead, which was familiar to Jacob. He stopped at Leah's tent as she was unpacking for the night's stop.

"I remember this place well," he told her. "Twenty years ago I stayed in this very spot. Tomorrow we can camp at a large valley just three days' journey from the Jordan River. I called it 'Mahanaim.' "

"Mahanaim? 'Double camp?' It must be a big place, then."

Jacob nodded. "Big enough to support us for a while. We can decide what to do about Esau—"

"Father! Mother!" Reuben rushed up to them. "Someone's coming! Look! Toward the east!"

Leah heard Jacob gasp. "What is it, Jacob?" she asked.

"It must be Laban!" Jacob's voice was anguished.

"Laban? Is he alone?"

"No, Mother," said Reuben. "It looks like at least fifty men—all armed! What shall we do?"

"He'll kill us all!" Jacob couldn't disguise his panic. "We can't possibly— Oh, Leah, what shall we do?"

Leah, too, had felt a sudden surge of panic. But her husband and her son had turned to her for help and advice. She took a deep breath. This was a time for clear and calm thinking.

"We have nothing to fear, Jacob." She wished she felt as sure of that as her voice sounded. "No harm will come to us. Remember, you're the heir of the Promise."

Jacob nodded, although Leah wasn't sure if his sudden composure was due to this reminder of God's protection or her own apparent calm.

"Do you think he'll attack?" he asked.

"No, I don't think so. He has always been afraid of our God. He'll probably want to talk first. You know how shrewd he is. He thinks he can get the better of anybody by smooth talk."

"But what does he want? Surely not our off-color livestock!"

"No," replied Leah. "But I have no idea what he wants. You'll have to talk to him. Just be careful. He'll try to trick you somehow."

"Mother," said Reuben, "they're setting up camp over there on the hill opposite ours. At least he's not going to attack right away!"

"He won't attack at all, son," said Leah, wishing she felt as sure of that as her tone implied.

When the evening sun shone weakly in the west, Laban and his five sons left the camp and marched down the hill, into the valley, and up the hill toward Jacob's camp. Jacob hurried to Leah's tent and told her they were coming.

She heard Laban herself, then. Laban had evidently stopped about halfway up the hillside and was calling on Jacob to come out and talk.

"Go to him, Jacob," said Leah. "But take only our five oldest boys. And send Naphtali to me." Naphtali was their sixth son.

"Why can't I go?" asked Naphtali as he hurried up to Leah. "I can fight as well as Dan!"

"They aren't going to fight, boy. They're going to talk. And your father must have the same number of sons as Laban."

"Oh. But what should *I* do?"

"Take me to the edge of the hill, so we can hear what's going on."

Naphtali obeyed, and they pushed through a flock of sheep and soon stood at the edge of the hill. Leah could feel the evening breeze on her face.

Below then there was only silence.

"What are they doing, Naphtali?" asked Leah.

"Nothing." The boy whispered. "They're just standing there, staring at each other!"

Leah nodded. Jacob would need his wits now. Evidently he was waiting for Laban—the aggressor—to speak first.

Laban was indeed the first to break the silence. "What do you mean by sneaking off like you did?" he demanded. "Are my daughters prisoners, captured in battle, that you have hustled them off like hostages? Why didn't you at least let me give them a farewell party, with singing and dancing? Why didn't you let me say good-bye to my grandchildren? You had no right to run off like that!"

Laban's voice was indignant, almost whining. Jacob's reply was stronger, more self-assured.

"Would you have let me go if I had asked you? Would you have let me take my wives and children and all my possessions?"

Leah nodded. She liked Jacob's tone of voice, as well as his biding for time by saying nothing important.

Menace underlay Laban's reply. "I could crush you now, but I won't. I will not fight against both your God and my teraphim!"

His answer was evidently as puzzling to Jacob as it was to Leah.

"What do you mean—both my God and your teraphim?"

Now Laban's reply was thunderous. "It wasn't enough for you to steal my daughters, my grandchildren, and my livestock. You had to steal my gods as well!"

Leah caught her breath. So that was it! His household gods were missing! No wonder he was so upset. No wonder he had come out on this long journey, with an army, prepared for trouble. His household teraphim! They were more important to him than his daughters, his grandchildren, and all his flocks and herds.

"I didn't steal your teraphim," said Jacob evenly. "A curse upon him who did! Let him die! Come and see for yourself. You and your sons may search my camp. Look among the flocks and herds. Look into every tent, every saddlebag. If you find one thing that belongs to you, you may take it back without question. Then the thief will die. I swear this before God and all these men!"

"Agreed!"

Naphtali whispered, "They're coming this way!"

Now Leah heard Laban's voice, much closer, as he spoke to his sons. "You take the flocks and servants. See if you can find any solid-color goats or sheep among them. And search the servants' belongings. I'll look in the tents."

Jacob then instructed his sons. "Tell everyone in camp to let Laban and his sons look anywhere they want. If they find anything belonging to them, bring to me whoever took it!"

Suddenly Leah began to tremble.

"What is it, Mother Leah?" asked Naphtali. "Are you all right?"

She took a deep breath, trying to calm herself. "Take me to your mother's tent. Now!"

Naphtali's mother was Rachel. Although he had

come from Bilhah's womb, he—and everyone else— considered him Rachel's son.

As they pushed through a herd of goats on their way to Rachel's tent, Leah was close to panic. What was Rachel thinking, to steal the teraphim? Didn't she realize what she had done? She was playing with the lives of everyone in the family!

But it would be worth the risk to Rachel. The teraphim meant everything to her. They meant controlling the family lineage, what Jacob called the "birthright"— the right of the oldest son to retain leadership in the family. Rachel must believe that with the teraphim she could ensure Joseph's becoming clan patriarch at Jacob's death. The teraphim would also bring her more children in the never-ceasing rivalry with her sister.

"Mother Leah!" whispered Naphtali. "It's Laban! He's coming this way!"

The crunch of Laban's sandals sounded angrily on the stony ground as he hurried from Leah's tent toward them. He passed by Leah without even speaking, and pushed into Rachel's tent.

Jacob hurried up to them. "Has he found anything yet?" he asked anxiously.

Leah shook her head, and they stood at the doorway to Rachel's tent, watching what was happening inside.

"Greetings, Father!" Rachel's voice was bright and cheerful. Leah imagined the dimples showing on her cheeks as she smiled. "It's good to see you again!"

Laban said nothing. He began a systematic search.

"It's good to have you in my tent, Father," said Rachel cheerfully. "Please forgive me for not getting up, but the time of the women is upon me."

Laban hesitated briefly at this but said nothing. He went about his work faster than usual, as though anxious to be gone from the tent. Leah knew he didn't like to be around a woman during these monthly periods.

Leah heard all this from the doorway of the tent. She knew Rachel was lying. It wasn't her time. Why was she saying this? Suddenly she knew.

"Where is your mother sitting?" she whispered to Naphtali.

"On the saddlebag," he replied, confused by her question.

So that's where the missing teraphim were! Laban would never look there. Not with Rachel sitting on it during her unclean time.

Laban, still saying nothing, came out of the tent, pushing past Jacob and Leah. One of Laban's sons came running up.

"We found nothing, Father," he said.

Laban turned to Jacob, but before he could speak, Jacob stepped forward.

"You didn't expect to find them, did you? Do you think I'm a common thief? Show me what you have found that belongs to you!"

Leah guessed what was behind her husband's diatribe. Jacob knew how Laban felt about the teraphim, and how powerless he must feel now without them. This was his chance, not only to vent his own feelings, but to attack.

Jacob wasn't finished. "Twenty years! Is that all twenty years mean to you? I've served you faithfully and honestly. The first fourteen years were for your two daughters; the last six were for myself. In all that time, I've been scrupulously honest. I took from you only the wages we agreed on. And I've built up *your* flocks and herds, too! I've done this with God's help—"

Here Jacob paused and took a deep breath before shouting, "With the help of the great God of my grandfather, Abraham, by the awesome God of my father,

Isaac. With the help of Almighty God, I have served you well for twenty years!"

Laban was now on the defensive. "Yes. You're right. I owe you an apology, Jacob. I mean no harm. How can I hurt my daughters and grandchildren?"

Leah smiled to herself. Not without your teraphim, she thought. She breathed easier.

Laban was backing away. "It's late. See, the sun has already set. We both need to have supper and rest. We can continue our discussion in the morning."

"What more do we have to talk about?" demanded Jacob.

"Tomorrow we'll declare a covenant between us. We'll set up a pillar to God commemorating our friendship.

Jacob was silent for a moment before replying. "All right. Tomorrow. Just you and your sons. Your army shall stay in their camps."

"Agreed."

Laban and his sons turned and marched off.

Darkness settled on the camp. The cooking fires weren't lit yet; there had been too much excitement for anyone to think about that. Leah sensed that everyone was breathing easier. Surely they would all feel Jacob had won the confrontation, and tomorrow would bring more victories for their household.

But Leah wasn't so sure. She knew how shrewd her father was. What did he want?

"Take me to my tent, Naphtali," she said.

"Don't bother." Jacob stood beside her. "I'll take her."

He grasped Leah's arm and led her toward her tent. "I want to talk with you."

Leah nodded. She was proud of her husband, and the way he had handled things today. She would tell him so. And they would plan for tomorrow.

She smiled. Jacob wouldn't spend the night in Rachel's tent tonight. He had heard Rachel's lie about her "time of the women." Just as well. They needed to talk.

7

"What does he want now, Leah?"

Jacob leaned forward slightly as he sat on the carpet in Leah's tent. Outside they could smell the savory odors of many cooking pots. The entire camp was busy, settling in for a long stay on this hilltop.

Leah sat beside him. Beside her, Dinah slept peacefully on the carpet.

She looked at her husband thoughtfully. "I think he wants your God."

"What!" Jacob leaned back and stared at her. Then suddenly he grinned. "Of course! That has to be it! I wonder what happened to his teraphim?"

May you never find out, thought Leah. Aloud she said, "He probably thinks God destroyed them. You know how he feels about your God. He must think God is indeed powerful to come into the land of Haran—the homeland of his teraphim—and completely vanquish them."

Jacob snorted. "Well, he's right about that. Those silly pieces of wood he thinks are gods haven't done much for him these past twenty years."

"And that's why my father wants your God," said Leah.

"Does he think God is something he can buy or take by force, or maybe steal from me?"

"Why not? That's the way he feels about the teraphim."

Jacob was silent for a moment. Finally he said, "Then tomorrow he'll try to take God away from me. What do you think he'll do? Offer to buy God? Take God by force? He should know I'd never sell God even if I could, and there's no way God would let him defeat us even with his big army. So what's left? Treachery?"

Leah nodded. "That's Father's strong point. Why not?"

Jacob laughed. "If that's true, then we have nothing to worry about. He must have a very cheap opinion of God if he can think that. But then, that's the way his teraphim would be. This whole business tomorrow could be very funny."

"No. It's not at all funny. It's dangerous." Leah reached out and touched her husband's hand. "You must be careful, Jacob. It's all very childish to you, but not to him. Remember, he was brought up thinking that way. If he even thinks God has left you and come over to his side, do you realize what that could mean?"

The smile faded from Jacob's face. "Yes," he said slowly. "Then my job tomorrow is to see that Laban doesn't *think* my God has deserted me. How can I do that?"

"You'll find a way." Leah squeezed Jacob's hand. "I believe in you. And in our God."

Jacob's response was to hold her hand for a moment. "Thanks, Leah. I feel better." He stood. "I'd better check the guards. They might be asleep." He grinned. "Not that it will make any difference. God is the only guard we'll need tonight!"

"Will you be coming back to my tent tonight?"

Jacob shook his head. "It's almost time for Dinah to

71

wake up and cry for her supper. You know how I feel about crying girl-babies. I'll eat supper in Rachel's tent tonight."

"But she's—" She dropped her eyes. She was about to say it was Rachel's unclean time, but she couldn't lie to her husband. Not even for a night of love with him.

Jacob stepped closer to her and put his arm around her shoulder. "I know, Leah. I understand."

He turned her to him, then with his other hand he lifted her chin so that he could look into her eyes. Leah was aware of tears forming in them.

"We have so much together," he said gently. "I think you know how much you mean to me. You've given me my sons, and you've shared your counsel with me. What we have between us is very special."

Leah's eyes overflowed, and she put her head on his shoulder. But he gently turned her face up and kissed her on the lips. "Be at peace, my love." Then with a final embrace, he turned and left the tent.

Leah sank to the carpet. Was he really expressing, in his own way, his love? Or was it just gratitude? Gratitude for her counsel, motherhood, companionship?

She knew the answer. In spite of his mistaken belief that Rachel was in her unclean time, he would spend the night with her. In fact, he would probably find out she wasn't unclean. Would he guess the reason for her lie? Or would he be too preoccupied with her to care?

The tears came unchecked, and she buried her head in her hands.

The next morning at sunrise, Jacob and his sons stood on the edge of the hillside and watched the signs of activity in the camp opposite. Leah stood just behind them, holding Dinah in her arms. Naphtali again stood beside her to act as her eyes.

"What are they doing now, boy?" she asked.

72

"I don't know."

"Well, tell me what you see."

"I see Laban and his five sons. They're working with ropes and—" He stared. "I think it's a big log. But it's too heavy to be a log. Probably a stone. Yes, that's it. A big stone."

"How big?"

Naphtali shrugged. "I don't know. Maybe if I stood beside it, it would come to my waist at the biggest part. I couldn't reach around it."

Leah tried to picture the rock from the boy's inadequate description. There were many such stones in the area. It was probably smooth, cylindrical, and larger at one end than at the other.

"What are they doing with it?"

"I think they're trying to slide it down the hillside."

"Ah, I see." She almost laughed aloud at what she had just said. She *could* see it, in her mind. The five stalwart young men and their aged father, working with ropes, trying to slide the huge stone down the hill without cracking it. But why?

Naphtali pulled on Leah's sleeve. "Laban's coming down the hill ahead of his sons. He's standing at the foot of the hill now."

Then Leah heard her father's voice clearly. "May your God give you a good day, Jacob. I trust you slept well last night."

Jacob replied cautiously, "Yes, thank you."

Laban's voice was smooth. "I hope you won't mind if I invite you and your five sons to come down into the valley between us. As you see, this pillar is too heavy to haul up to your camp. We can set it up down here, can't we?"

"And what is the pillar for, Laban? A pact of friendship and peace between us?"

"Of course. We'll seal it by each of us offering a sacrifice to God on it."

Leah's mind whirled. What was her father up to? Somehow he would try to entice Jacob's God away from him and into his camp. Could he be thinking that by offering a larger, more expensive sacrifice, God would be impressed and go over to him?

Jacob laughed. He was probably thinking the same thing. He must be warned.

"Be careful, Jacob," she whispered from behind him. "To you this is silly, but not to him. If he even thinks he has taken your God from you, he might try to kill us all."

Jacob nodded, suddenly sobering. "I have an idea." He turned to his five sons. "Each of you pick up a rounded stone, as big as you can carry. Bring it with you as we go down into the valley."

Leah smiled, admiring her husband's strategy. Laban would set up his pillar, but Jacob would build a cairn of rocks beside it. And because Jacob's would consist of many small stones, he could pile on as many as needed. He could easily build a taller cairn than Laban's pillar.

"What are they doing now?" she asked Naphtali.

"Well, I see those five sons of Laban putting the big stone in the ground. It looks like a table. And now my brothers are piling up their stones beside it. They're getting more stones to put on top."

"How far apart are they?"

"Are what, Mother Leah?"

Patience, she told herself. "Laban's pillar and your father's pile of stones."

"Oh. About ten paces."

There was silence down below, and Leah could imagine the two sides standing beside their own altar

74

glaring at each other. *Careful, Jacob!* she thought.

"Now let us make a sacrifice," said Laban.

"No." Jacob's answer was firm. "There will be no sacrifice. Only a watchtower, so that God will keep watch between us."

Again there was silence between them. Finally Laban sighed. "This place shall be called 'Jegar-sahadutha,' " he said.

Leah caught her breath. *Jegar-sahadutha* meant "witness post" in the language the people of Haran spoke. An innocent name, but the language made the difference. Laban must think God would come over to his side if they named the place in Haran's language.

Jacob spoke then, his voice strong. "It shall be called 'Galeed,' " he said.

Leah felt like cheering. Her husband had seen the trap Laban had set for him. In Jacob's language, *Galeed* meant "witness pile." Only a slight difference, apart from the language. But an important one.

Again the silence was so strong, Leah could almost feel it. When Laban finally spoke, his voice was resigned.

"Let it be called 'Mizpah.' "

The word was common to both languages, and meant only "watching place." It could refer to either the pillar or the pile of stones, or both. But it couldn't apply to one and not the other.

"Mizpah," said Jacob, confirming the name.

"Then let us make a covenant here," said Laban. "May God watch between us while we're absent from each other."

"Agreed," said Jacob. Then he added, "Mizpah."

But Laban wasn't finished. "This pillar is called upon to witness that God will follow you wherever you go, and if you ever do harm to my daughters, or marry another in their place, God will punish you accordingly. Mizpah."

"Mizpah," said Jacob.

That was easy enough to agree to, thought Leah. Jacob never mistreated his wives and would never marry again. He needed no more sons and had all his needs, both physical needs and the need for companionship, satisfied by Rachel and Leah. This covenant was easy.

But what else was he up to?

Her mind went back over her father's words. One phrase jumped out at her. "God will follow you wherever you go," Laban had said. That could only mean one thing: Laban believed he had not stolen Jacob's God.

As though to confirm her thought, Laban continued. "This pile of stones and this pillar stand as a boundary line between us. Neither of us shall cross beyond this place into the other's territory while we live. After we die, our descendants shall not cross. May God watch between us while we are absent, to make sure we do not. Mizpah."

"Mizpah," agreed Jacob.

But Laban still wasn't finished. "I will call upon the God of our fathers, the God of Abraham and Nahor, and their common ancestor, Terah, to be the witness between us. Mizpah."

The words caught Leah by surprise. God was the God of Abraham and Isaac, but not of Nahor and Terah. Did Laban not know this? Or did his words mean he now believed God was the God of both branches of the family?

"Mizpah!" said Jacob firmly. "May God watch between us while we are apart from each other. May the all-powerful God of my father, Isaac, the all-seeing God of Abraham, the God in whose hand is life and death—may this awesome God keep our covenant between us. May he destroy me—or you—if either of us ever steps over this boundary line again. Mizpah!"

Jacob spoke his final words loudly and with ringing conviction. They had their desired effect on Laban.

"Mizpah," said Laban softly.

It was over, then. Leah heard Jacob and their sons scrambling up the hillside toward them. She didn't need Naphtali's urgent whisper, "They're coming back!"

The next instant Jacob stood before her, breathing hard after his quick climb. He grasped both her hands.

"We did it, Leah! We're safe!"

"We are indeed!" Leah smiled at him. "You were magnificent, Jacob! I couldn't be more proud of you!"

"Nor I of you. Hurry! I must tell Rachel the news. Let's offer a sacrifice and have a family celebration. Tomorrow morning, you and Rachel and the children can say good-bye to Laban. Then we'll break camp and go home."

Home! He meant the land of Canaan, of course. Not Haran. That would never be her home again. She could never cross that invisible boundary line at the foot of the hill.

Nor did she want to. Her home was with Jacob.

8

"What do you see, Jacob?"

The sun shone warmly on Leah's face as she spoke. She wondered if the early morning glare would bother Jacob's view as he faced the east where Laban's army was encamped. Earlier that morning, Jacob had sent his wives and children, two at a time, down into the valley to the Mizpah boundary line. There, Laban had kissed them and bade them farewell.

Now the camp behind them was quiet. Jacob had sent his flocks and herds out in small droves, seeking their own pasture and water, in a slow migration toward their next rendezvous. The grass was almost completely gone from the small mountaintop where they had encamped for the past three days while dealing with Laban.

"Laban is leaving." Jacob described the orderly procession of Laban, his sons, and small army of men, as they marched out of their camp, down the hillside, going east toward Haran. Laban was careful to skirt the invisible boundary line running north-south from the valley of the pillar and pile of stones.

"We're safe from them, Leah. He won't dare harm us now."

"I'm not sure he ever intended us harm," said Leah. "His whole purpose in following us was to find a god to worship. He couldn't get his teraphim back, so he took our God. I think he's well satisfied."

"Do you think he believes God is with him now?"

"I feel sure of it. He thinks God is with both your family and his."

"How do you know that?"

Leah paused. She recalled the scene yesterday in the valley, when the two shrewd men—her husband and her father—had faced each other in a battle of wits. Two very clever men, with devious minds, trying to outmaneuver each other. And they had both won. Both had received what they wanted: Laban, a God; and Jacob, his security.

She brought her mind back to Jacob's question, realizing he was still waiting for her answer. "Do you recall what my father said about the God of his father, Nahor?"

Jacob nodded. "He said God was the God of Nahor and Abraham and Terah. But he was mistaken, surely. God came to my grandfather, Abraham, and not to Laban's grandfather, Nahor. And our common ancestor, Terah of Ur, knew nothing of this God."

"And you, of course, were quick to point out to him that God is the God of your father, Isaac, and your grandfather, Abraham. He didn't even argue with you. He has accepted in his own mind that God is now the God of all the descendants of Terah."

Jacob sighed. "Well, it doesn't matter much whether he thinks God is now his God, as long as he respects our covenant and leaves us alone. I don't want anything more to do with that sneaky old man."

It occurred to Leah that Laban probably felt the same way about Jacob. But then another thought followed. How would her father adapt to this new God of his? All his life he had worshiped a god who lived in a piece of wood, who could be bought and appeased with gifts, who was susceptible to flattery, who played favorites.

Laban's new God would be different. Could Laban adjust to an invisible God? Would God tolerate Laban's type of worship? Would Laban be looking for good luck—an immediate upturn in his fortunes? For a fleeting moment, Leah wished she could help her father adjust, at least for a little while. She and Jacob could help him to understand, to adapt to this new approach to religion, to appreciate the value of this new faith.

Jacob's words interrupted her train of thought. "We must move on. When we get to Mahanaim, we'll set up two camps. You and your family will occupy the northern valley, and Rachel and her family the south. The flocks and herds will be divided equally. We can stay there for a while, until we're ready."

"Ready for what, Jacob?" Leah felt she knew the answer to her question.

"Esau." Jacob's somber tone reflected his concern. "What are we going to do about him?"

Leah considered this for a moment as Jacob led her to her tent. "Why not send a messenger to your brother and tell him you're coming?"

"But why should we do that? Shouldn't we try to slip into the land of Canaan unobserved, and then consolidate our strength before he finds us? Why tell him now?"

"It might be better for him to receive friendly word directly from you that you're here, rather than hear it from someone else. He might hear that you're coming against him with an army, looking for a fight."

"But Leah, we're not!"

"That's why it's better for us to send word to him we're coming as a peaceful brotherly family."

Jacob nodded. "I'll send Omri. He's the one person who can memorize a message from us and present it in a friendly way. If anyone can make a favorable impression, Omri can."

"Good choice. And ask him to find out if your mother is still alive."

They had reached Leah's tent. All around her, servants hurried and bustled, dismantling the camp in preparation for travel. There was much to do. Much for Jacob to do. Yet he stayed for a moment, wanting to say something more. Leah sensed his hesitancy.

"What is it, Jacob?" she asked.

"Leah. . . . " Jacob gasped her hand. Leah waited while he gathered his thoughts. "Leah, if anything happens to me, if I'm killed—"

Leah caught her breath. The words rushed to her lips, but she fought them down. She wanted to tell him that everything would be all right, that nothing would happen to him. But she knew she would be saying that only for her own peace of mind. He must have his say.

"If I'm killed," Jacob continued, "you'll take care of my sons, won't you?"

What was he saying? Of course she would take care of his children. He knew that. She felt a rush of warmth and tenderness for her husband, who would turn to her with this request, so deeply important for him. Was he saying merely that he trusted her—above all others—to give leadership to a suddenly leaderless family? Or was there something else?

And then she knew what it was.

"If you're killed, Jacob—God forbid—then I'll look after your family." She paused, looking up at him, her eyes wide, telling him through her glance that she meant what she said. Then she added slowly, "*All* your family."

Jacob relaxed, the tension escaping from him in a long sigh. He knew, then, what she meant. *All* his family. That included Joseph. *Especially* Joseph.

"Thank you, Leah," he muttered. Then he squeezed her hands.

Leah moved closer to Jacob, so her face was just a few inches from his. She looked at him, seeing the familiar face, slightly blurred but visible at this close range. She looked into his eyes.

"Jacob," she said, and was surprised at how calm her voice was. "Do you plan to give Joseph the blessing for the birthright?"

Jacob didn't move. His eyes bored into hers. For a long moment he didn't speak.

When he finally spoke, he whispered. "Yes." One word. But it pierced her as a sword.

Deep within her, forces struggled to possess her. She wouldn't let them. With a wrenching effort, she pushed them aside.

Leah smiled. "It shall be as you say," she said.

Jacob let his breath out in a rush. "Leah. . . . " He gripped her hands more tightly. "Leah. . . ." Then suddenly his arms were around her, and he pressed her to him.

When he finally was able to speak, he said, "Thank you, Leah. You do understand."

She had won her battle with herself, so she was able to smile. She looked up into his eyes and said, "I do understand. And don't worry. Joseph is—and will always be—the birthright son."

He kissed her tenderly on the forehead. "Thank you, Leah," he murmured. Then he released her and turned to go.

As his sandals crunched on the gravel ground, she stood still amidst the turmoil of travel preparations around her. She had given him a promise. An important promise. A painful promise.

Did he know what that promise had meant to her? Surely he did. That was why he hesitated to ask. But he had asked, and she had promised. She set her lips tightly. Yes, she would fulfill that promise—not just if Jacob were to die, but now, while he lived. She would accept Joseph as the favorite son. She would give him the honors of the birthright. Above Reuben. Above all the others. Because Jacob had asked, and she had promised.

And she would do it cheerfully.

9

Leah had given Jacob her promise to accept Joseph not only as the favorite but also as the heir of the birthright. It had been fairly easy—when Jacob held her in his arms. But, as Leah discovered during the next two weeks while they journeyed from Mizpah to Mahanaim, she had to fight the battle deep inside herself over and over.

Once, when Jacob stood beside Rachel's camel and held the baby Joseph for a moment before handing him up to Rachel for the day's travel, Leah overheard Jacob talking to his youngest son.

"My son," he had murmured. "My only son."

Inside her, she knew she was under attack again. The familiar conflict churned furiously. She could barely muster enough strength to fight it. She thought of Reuben, the firstborn, so deserving, so faithful. And so cheated. It was unfair. It was unjust. It was outrageous.

Suddenly she thought of Esau. The same thing had happened to him. Had he felt the same way? Of course he had! Leah could appreciate the holy oath which erupted from Esau's lips many years ago, an oath which might still bind him after so many years.

What could she do? Make a sacred vow of her own? Call on God to curse Joseph, to return the birthright to the person to whom it belonged? No. Such vows were foolish, born in the emotion of the moment, conceived in hate and anger. How could such a vow be binding? Surely God wouldn't hold a person to it. Not the God to whom Jacob had introduced her!

Leah lifted her head and took a deep breath. She was Jacob's wife. Everything in her background and heritage had told her to accept the will of her husband as the unquestioned law in the family. She must accept. She *must*! She had given Jacob her promise, and *that* promise was binding. And she had vowed to accept it cheerfully.

She wondered many times during the trek to Mahanaim whether some of her inner conflict showed through her expressive eyes. Rachel never suspected, she was sure. She was too happy, too involved in Jacob's love for her and his acceptance of Joseph as the heir of the Promise to notice anything. Jacob had seemed more tender toward Leah these past two weeks, perhaps from guilty feelings, perhaps sensing the depths of her agony. But he had said nothing.

Nor would Leah. She had accepted. She must thrust the hurt and jealousy and bitterness aside. She would— she *must*—smile.

Mahanaim was well named: "Two Camps." The broad valley had plenty of pasture and water. Jacob proceeded to divide his company into "two camps." Half went to the northern spring, half to the southern. Leah surveyed the cluster of tents at the northern spring and marveled at Jacob's wisdom. Not only were half the flocks and herds here, but also all her sons. The other half of the livestock was encamped with Rachel and her sons.

Jacob appeared at her tent the morning after their arrival at Mahanaim. For years this had been his custom. She had always treasured their few early morning moments together. She marveled that he still wanted to do this. After spending the night in Rachel's tent, he had walked almost a mile to keep his morning rendezvous with her.

"Walk with me, Leah," he said. "We can walk to the spring, as we used to do in Haran."

She smiled and took his sleeve. The morning conversations evidently meant as much to him as to her.

"Why don't you come into the tent and see your daughter?" Leah tried to keep her voice lighthearted. "You haven't held Dinah for a while."

Jacob's laugh was soft. "You know I don't like girl-babies. They're not the same as boy-babies."

"Really? They all do the same things. They eat at the same place. They cry and laugh and sleep—whether they're boys or girls."

"Now you know that's not true." The laughter was plain in his voice. "Girl-babies are always crying at one end and wetting at the other."

Leah laughed. "Boy-babies do that too. Or hadn't you noticed? You have such a prejudice against girls. But I suppose that's to be expected, after having eleven boys."

"Eleven boys!" Jacob always spoke enthusiastically when contemplating his wealth, and eleven sons were very much part of that wealth. They ranged in age from Reuben, just turning fourteen, to Joseph, only a few months old. They had come from the wombs of four women, although technically they were claimed by his two wives. But they were all his and would bring him much comfort in old age.

"Eleven boys and one girl," Leah said gently.

"All right. Eleven boys and one girl. But the girl can't begin to be compared with the eleven boys. Especially Joseph. Yes. Especially Joseph."

Leah was silent for a moment as she fought once again her battle. But she had won the war long before now. And it was easier when she walked beside her husband.

Was he saying that to be cruel? No. Impossible. Jacob was never cruel to her. But he was certainly reminding her of his favorite. And that reminded her of her promise.

She smiled at him. "Yes, Jacob. Especially Joseph."

"Leah." Jacob's voice was soft, the laughter gone from it. "I want you to know—"

Something was happening. Something in the center of the valley. Shouts. Hoofbeats. A rider on a camel.

"What is it, Jacob?"

"It's Omri. We'll know something now."

Omri was the servant they had sent to Esau with a message of peace and brotherly love. He had a good camel and had been gone only two weeks.

The camel hoofbeats approached. In her blurred vision, Leah could see the huge beast and its rider, heard their gasping breaths, and knew they had had a long hard ride.

"Welcome to Mahanaim. May God give you good health and a comfortable rest among us." Jacob spoke the ritual greeting to Omri. It was more than he needed to say to a servant, but it reflected Jacob's respect and affection for this man who had served him so well for the past ten years. "Get down and drink from the spring before you tell us your news."

"Thank you, Jacob." Omri dismounted while Jacob held the camel's reins. The beast was eager to drink, but Jacob held it firmly until Omri had refreshed himself.

When Omri stood up, his face and short black beard dripping with water, Jacob released the camel, which noisily buried its head in the water. Its drink would be long, and the little pond was immediately disturbed and muddy. An hour would pass before humans could drink there again.

"God be with you, Jacob." Omri, like everyone else, had accepted Jacob's God, although for him it was still "Jacob's God." But the ritual greeting required that God's name be used.

"I bring you news of your brother Esau, whom I finally found in Edom in the land of Seir to the south. I gave him your message of brotherly love and friendship."

"How did he receive it?"

"I couldn't tell. He said nothing, and his face reflected no emotion whatever. I don't know whether he was pleased or angry."

"Did he treat you well?"

Omri nodded. "He extended to me the traditional hospitality, inviting me to stay in his tents and eat with him for two nights and the day in between. I did, but I didn't see him after I first met him."

Jacob shuffled his feet. "Is he going to wait for me to come to see him?"

Omri shook his head vigorously. "He is *not*! I learned from one of his servants that he was recruiting a small army and getting ready to travel."

"An army!"

"Yes. I couldn't find out how many, but I know they are armed. They have bows and arrows."

Leah caught her breath. She knew that the bow and arrow were Esau's weapons. He would have taught his men how to use them well.

"When is he coming?" Jacob's voice reflected his anxiety.

"I don't know. On the morning my hospitality invitation was over, I mounted my camel and rode it fast as I could."

"Thank you, Omri. You've done well."

"What shall we do, Jacob? He'll kill us all!" Omri had obviously been fretting about this during his long hot ride from Edom to Mahanaim.

"He'll not harm us, my friend." Jacob's voice was calm, but Leah recognized the tremor in it, barely concealed from his servant. "Remember, God is on our side."

"God be praised," muttered Omri, but his voice lacked enthusiasm. He had lived too long with impotent idols to put much faith in any deity.

"Omri," Jacob said slowly, "Did you learn anything about my mother?"

Omri nodded solemnly. "She's dead, Jacob. She died four years ago. Esau was with her."

Jacob frowned, but said nothing. It seemed to Leah the news was what he expected. He showed no grief.

Omri dragged his camel from the water and led him away. When he had gone, Jacob turned to Leah.

"First Laban. Now Esau. We're trapped again!"

Leah grasped her husband's sleeve and they walked back toward her tent. "Don't forget, Laban came with no intention of harming you. Maybe it's the same with Esau. Maybe he only wants to greet his long-lost brother."

"With a group of armed men? No. I think Esau is a vicious killer who wouldn't hesitate to kill us all. He swore an oath, remember. And Esau isn't the type to change his ways."

"But don't forget what you told Omri. God is with you. You are the heir to the birthright. God will protect you."

"I wish I could believe that!"

Leah cringed inside. Jacob's words were bitter, spoken with an edge of despair. It was as though his face were torn away, and she could see deep inside him. His outer faith and confidence were a mask!

During the twenty years she had been his wife, he had always appeared confident, his faith steady, a rock, never moving. Only rarely, as during that first week of their marriage, when he had spoken so confidentially to her of his faith, had she caught this glimpse of uncertainty.

She felt compelled to speak to him, to comfort him with words of assurance. She wanted to remind him of the birthright, of the dream he had had at Bethel, of the years of servitude under Laban when he had prospered, and of the more recent encounter with Laban at Mizpah. The words rushed to her lips, but before they could come out, he spoke.

"I know God is with me." Jacob's voice held anguish. "He has certainly proved that often enough. But I'm still not sure—"

Leah clutched her husband's arm. "You can never be sure, Jacob. Never. All you can do is believe."

He nodded. "If only I could meet God face-to-face. To speak to God. To have God personally bless me. But . . . God is not a person, like we are. I can never do that."

She nodded. "Yes. We have to believe without ever seeing God face-to-face."

Jacob took a deep breath. "But this doesn't solve our immediate problem, Leah. What are we going to do?"

An idea leaped into Leah's mind. She wondered if the same thing had occurred to her husband when he had divided the camp.

"We must split up, Jacob. Rachel's clan should go south, and I'll take my clan north. Then, if he finds one part of your family and destroys it, the other half will survive. Isn't that why you divided the family when we came to Mahanaim?"

Jacob stopped, turned to her, and looked into her face. "I wish I could say yes, but that wasn't the reason. It was—but never mind that now. You're right. Let's begin right now. Who knows how much time we have?"

Jacob's quick mind grasped the plan, and details tumbled from him. Leah listened, glad that her husband had something to occupy his mind. The northern half of the family, Leah's half, would cross the Jabbok River and encamp in the hills. The southern half, Rachel's, would go into the desert to the south. Esau would come to Mahanaim first, and then he must decide which trail to follow.

"I'll go with Rachel," he said. "Then I can protect Rachel and Joseph."

Leah shook her head. "He won't stop until he finds you, Jacob. If you're with Rachel, you'll only endanger her and her family."

"You're right. But if I go with you, you'll be in danger."

"Why not go off by yourself, then? Lose yourself in the hills?"

"I could do that. Nobody, not even the great hunter Esau, could find me in these hills. But if I do that, won't my brother hunt up both your camp and Rachel's, looking for me? Why put both families in danger—"

"Then leave a trail for him to follow."

Jacob stared at her, his face perplexed. Leah continued.

"When Esau arrives in Mahanaim, he'll study the tracks and learn about the division in your family. But if he finds the trail of one man going off by himself, he'll follow that. After all, it's you he wants, not your family."

Jacob nodded. "Yes. That's true. And I know this country, even better than he does. It's wild. There are caves and canyons and forests. Even if Esau has a big army, they'll never find me. And while they're looking for me, you'll be safe."

"Then let's get started."

They plunged into feverish activity. Jacob went to Rachel's tents first, while Leah began to organize her side of the family's move. She sent riders out to her sons and servants who were with the herds and flocks. Then she supervised the job of packing the tents.

In the late afternoon, Jacob returned. He had already sent Rachel off toward the south.

"I'll go with you as far as the Jabbok River," he said. "I want to find the ford. It's the only place you can cross with all the livestock."

They arrived at the river just before sunset and pushed on to cross the river before dark. Jacob told them of a place about a mile away where they could camp for the night.

Then it was time to say good-bye.

Jacob embraced Leah. She felt the strength of his arms around her. Perhaps for the last time. No. She mustn't think like that. It was only a temporary parting.

But the enthusiasm of his embrace warmed her. Surely he hadn't said farewell to Rachel with any more emotion and affection than he gave her. He kissed her lips, and the kiss was long and lingering. He spoke no words, but the embrace was enough.

Then he was gone, and she felt suddenly alone. The darkness settled around her as she mounted her camel and was led toward the mountain glen, where they would camp for the night. They still had several hours of work ahead, setting up camp. She would work at it hard, trying to stave off the loneliness following Jacob's parting.

But never had she felt more alone.

10

Leah woke abruptly in the early morning. Something was wrong. She had been dreaming but couldn't remember what about except that it had left her with a strange uneasiness and foreboding. The darkness of the tent did nothing to dispel the heavy feeling of disaster pressing on her.

She got up and made her way to the doorway of the tent. Outside all was quiet. The gray mist of dawn was just beginning to absorb the black smudge of night. Soon the camp would be stirring, but now all was quiet. Even the silence deepened her feeling that something dreadful was happening.

She told herself this was silly. Everything was all right. She was worried, that's all. Worried because Esau was coming. Esau, with an army of men behind him and hatred in his heart. Esau, whose birthright had been snatched away by his scheming brother many years ago. Leah shivered in the chilly air.

Still the feeling of impending disaster clung to her. Something was wrong. Her rational mind and common sense couldn't deny it.

She stumbled back into the tent and fumbled in the darkness until she found one of the sleeping boys. She shook him awake.

"What is it, Mother?" It was Issachar, three years

old, his voice blurred with sleep.

"Go to Reuben's tent, son. Tell him I must see him immediately. It's important."

The boy threw off his blanket and stumbled naked out of the tent, sleep still fogging his mind. The cold air would soon wake him up. Leah nodded her head. He obeyed. His obedience was unquestioning, a trait which had been ingrained in all eleven of Jacob's sons since birth.

Leah made her way to the doorway of the tent. In no time Reuben was before her. "What is it, Mother?" The concern in his voice touched her. She was acting irrationally, she knew; Reuben had a right to be concerned.

"Reuben, I want you to do something for me without questioning it. Please rouse one of your brothers and ride to the ford of the Jabbok River where we left your father yesterday. See if he's all right."

"But Mother, he won't be there. He'll be back in the hills somewhere, and we'd never find him. Are *you* all right, Mother?"

"I'm all right. Just do as I say. If you don't find him at the ford, come back immediately."

"All right, Mother." Reuben turned to go. For fourteen years he had obeyed his mother and he did it instinctively now. She wondered if he would have obeyed Jacob as readily.

What she had asked him to do would take only a short time. He would be back before the camp was fully awake.

Leah settled herself on the carpet just outside the door of the tent, huddling in a blanket to keep warm. She heard Reuben rouse one of his brothers in a nearby tent. The boy grumbled at being wakened so early. A moment later she heard the hoofbeats of the camels as they plodded off down the hillside. The boys were sensibly walking the camels in the semidarkness; they would ride them back later in the daylight.

Waiting was the hardest part. She wished she could go herself. But that would be foolish. She was blind and would be more hindrance than help. She would have to wait.

The morning hadn't fully arrived when she heard the hoofbeats of a camel riding fast up the hill and into the camp. She stood to receive its rider, who came directly to her tent.

"Mother! Father has had a terrible accident!" It was Simeon, her second son.

The news didn't surprise her. It was what she had expected.

"Tell me what you found, son." Her words were calm, despite her inner turmoil. Her calmness seemed to steady the thirteen-year-old boy.

"When we came over the hill just above the ford, we could see him lying face down on a rock on the other side of the river. His leg looked twisted. Reuben sent me back immediately, while he went on to him."

Leah nodded. "Go rouse Levi and Judah. Have them get their camels and meet us at the ford. Then come back here. I want to ride with you on your camel."

Simeon turned and ran. She could hear the excited sounds from the nearby tent, as Simeon told his brothers the news. Then he was back. "They'll meet us at the ford, Mother."

"Help me mount the camel, son."

Awkwardly she mounted the kneeling camel, still clutching the blanket which had kept her warm while she waited. Simeon slid into the cleft in front of her. She held onto him as he urged the beast to a cautious speed down the hillside.

No one questioned that she should go. Everyone knew she was the person most qualified to handle Jacob's injury. She had had much experience ever since her mother had died; everyone had turned to her when there was sickness or injury. Though her eyesight prevented her from seeing clearly, her sensitive hands and ears had learned to diagnose a problem by touch and sound. For twenty-five years she had been setting bones, closing wounds, and cooling fevers.

The camel splashed through the shallow water of the Jabbok River. Then Reuben was there, holding the camel's head and making it kneel. Simeon dismounted first and helped her down. Reuben took her arm and led her to Jacob's side.

Jacob was lying face down on the rock, but he was conscious. "Leah!" he gasped through his pain.

"I'm here, my husband."

She said no more, but her hands began a careful survey of his body. When she came to his hip, he tensed, and she knew that here was the problem. He gasped while her fingers gently probed the area of the hip joint. She let out her breath slowly. The leg wasn't broken. It was just out of joint.

"I can fix it," she said. "I'll do it now."

Reuben knelt beside her. "Mother, there's something you must know. There's a man around here somewhere. Father told me he fought with him."

Again that feeling of foreboding gripped her. "Who was it? Esau?"

"I don't know, Mother."

"*It was God!*"

The words came with a gasp from Jacob. He twisted his head to talk with them, and even this slight movement seemed to bring pain to his body. "I wrestled with God during the night. God . . . blessed me!"

"I understand, my husband." She said the words more to soothe him than to express what she believed. She no more understood his statement than she knew why the feeling of impending disaster suddenly left her, leaving in its place a strange peace.

"I'll take care of your leg now." Her voice was surprisingly steady. She turned to her four sons, for Levi and Judah had just joined them. "Reuben, hold his other leg. Levi and Judah, take his shoulders and arms. Hold him steady. If he tries to struggle, hold him as still as you can."

This was a difficult assignment for these boys. Levi and Judah were only eleven and ten, but they took their places.

"Just a moment, Mother." Reuben was gone briefly, but he returned almost immediately with a twig which he placed in Jacob's mouth. "Bite on this, Father," he said.

Leah knew what she had to do. She placed her foot on his buttocks, feeling gently for a firm footing. Then she grasped his ankle.

"Are you ready, Jacob?"

"My name isn't Jacob!" The words came out around the stick held in his teeth. They were garbled but understandable. "Don't call me Jacob anymore. I am *Israel*!"

She had no time to be surprised at this bizarre statement. "It shall be as you say, Israel," she said. Then she pulled on his leg as hard as she could.

There was a hideous snap in the hip joint, and Jacob gave a strangled cry. His body jerked. Then he fainted.

Leah's sensitive fingers probed the hip joint. "It's done," she said. "Now hand me the girdle he was wearing."

As gently as possible she slipped the long cloth belt

under his body and tied it firmly around his hips. Then she bound his legs at the knees with the cord of his headpiece. She bound his feet together with another cord. She hoped it would immobilize him enough so the bone wouldn't slip out of place again.

She could relax now. She leaned back against a rock with a sigh of relief. But Reuben wouldn't let her rest.

"Mother, what shall we do?"

Leah didn't answer him immediately. Instead, she smiled at him, hoping it would ease the tension she sensed in his body. How like his father he was! In time of crisis he turned to her for help. Reuben had done it all his life; Jacob had just begun to do it in recent years. It had taken him a long time to accept her as an equal, trusting her judgment and advice.

When she finally answered Reuben, her voice was firm. "We shall go to Mahanaim."

"Mahanaim! But Mother, Esau will surely find us there."

"Yes, he will." She smiled at him again, and was surprised that she actually felt the confidence and peace she wanted to communicate to him.

"But Mother! He'll kill us all!"

"He will *not* kill us, son. You will see."

The boy was silent for a moment. He did *not* see. But she knew the thought of disobedience would never cross his mind.

"All right, Mother," he mumbled.

"Boys, come here." She stood up as her four sons gathered around her. "This is what we'll do. Judah, go back to camp and tell them to pack up and go to Mahanaim. Now. Today. Levi, go to Rachel's tents, and tell her the same thing. Reuben and Simeon, help me rig a litter for your father. We'll carry him to Mahanaim from here."

The boys were silent for a moment. Would they obey her? Then Reuben spoke. "All right, Mother." The boys went off on their assignments.

Leah smiled to herself, marveling at the confidence her sons placed in her. Marveling also at her own inner calm. The feeling of foreboding which had wakened her this morning was gone. It had left her abruptly the moment Jacob had announced his new name was "Israel." Strange. What—

"Mother, how shall we build the litter?"

Reuben's question brought her back to the situation before her. "We'll need two long poles, son. And a blanket; use the one I brought. Now, here's what you must do. . . . "

11

Evening shadows crept across the valley at Mahanaim, and Leah could smell the night moisture thickening the air. Rachel's half of the family had just arrived, although Leah's half, led by young Judah, had come in midafternoon. The litter carrying Jacob had been there since midmorning, only a few hours after Leah had set the bone at the ford of the Jabbok.

Jacob was sleeping now, but for a while earlier he had been babbling about the man he had wrestled with at the Jabbok River. He insisted on being called by his new name and Leah complied. She not only wanted to keep him from being upset, which might cause him to twist and turn his body, but there was something more. It was the name itself.

Israel.

The name meant "God Wrestler." Jacob in his delirium had said that the stranger with whom he fought had given him the name. Jacob had mumbled something about wanting to know the stranger's name, but all the man had told him was that Jacob's own name would now be Israel. In naming him, however, the stranger had named himself. Jacob had wrestled with God.

Had he really? Leah didn't know. But she desperately wanted to believe it. She had glimpsed just yesterday something of Jacob's lifelong struggle with himself, his need to reach for a power beyond his own life. Jacob longed, desperately ached, for a face-to-face meeting with his God. It had happened to his grandfather, Abraham. In a way, it had happened to Jacob in his youth, when he dreamed of a ladder with God at the top. At the top—so far away. Jacob wanted more than that. Had it happened last night?

Or had he just fallen on a rock, and a combination of his pain and anxiety over Esau precipitated a nightmare in the darkness by the ford of the river Jabbok?

Leah turned away from these thoughts, leaving the sleeping Jacob in the tent while she went outside to find Reuben. Darkness had fallen, and the people were still erecting their tents and cooking suppers. She waited just outside the tent. Soon Reuben and Omri came.

Reuben made the first suggestion. "Let's send Esau a gift," he said. "Some sheep and goats and even some camels. It may soften his anger toward us."

"Good idea," said Omri. "We could send him twenty she-goats and two he-goats and the same number of ewes and rams. Then perhaps three camels, which would be a novelty to him, because he doesn't own any as far as I could tell. We might even include a cow and some asses. What do you think, Leah?"

Both Reuben and Omri fell silent, awaiting her decision. Now that Jacob wasn't available to lead, they had turned to her.

She spoke boldly. "Good idea, as far as it goes. But that's only a token gift. Why not a substantial one? It might impress Esau more."

"What do you suggest, Mother?"

"Two hundred she-goats and ewes, twenty he-goats and rams, thirty milk camels with their colts, forty cows, ten bulls, twenty she-asses and ten he-asses."

Both Reuben and Omri gasped. "But Leah," protested Omri, "that takes out about a third of Jacob's wealth. It's an exceptionally large gift."

"I believe Mother is right." Reuben spoke slowly. "If the gift isn't acceptable to him, he will take all our herds and flocks anyway, not to mention killing us all."

"Don't worry, son. That won't happen. Remember, God is working for us. God will keep us safe and restore everything to us and more. God always has."

"My lady, I admire your faith," Omri said. "I wish I had as much. But I will begin collecting those animals tomorrow morning early."

Leah sensed his relief. The servant was more comfortable carrying out plans already made than making them.

"And one more thing," Leah said. The two men waited. "Let each group of animals be separated by a distance between them. When they meet Esau, let the men driving the first group say to him, 'These belong to your servant Jacob. They are a present for his brother Esau! He is eagerly looking forward to meeting with you himself!' "

Although Leah couldn't see Omri, she knew by his voice that he was smiling when he said, "I'll take the first group myself. I'll say those words to him when each group of animals comes into his camp. By the time the last gift reaches him, he should be properly impressed. If that doesn't appease his anger, nothing will!"

The two men departed into the darkness, leaving Leah to herself. Strange. She thought of Reuben as a man. He was only fourteen, with no hair on his face. Yet he was a man. He reminded her of Jacob when he first came to Haran many years ago. The reminder was infinitely sweet.

She turned and reentered the tent. Jacob slept peacefully, his hip and leg securely bound. She had rolled up two carpets and placed them on either side of him to keep him from rolling over during the night.

She had done all she could. All that remained was for the "man" Jacob had fought to be with them the next day. No. Not Jacob. Israel. She smiled as she lay down beside her husband to sleep. Israel. He had finally met his God face-to-face.

The next morning, Leah knelt beside Jacob in the soft morning light. "Good morning, Leah," he said vigorously. "Did Rachel make it into camp all right last night?"

Leah controlled the jealousy surging once again. Hoping it wouldn't show in her eyes, she smiled broadly and replied, "She's safe and well, Israel, as we all are."

"I'm glad you remembered my new name."

"I'll always call you Israel, my husband. It's a good name."

"Yes."

Leah's fingers probed into the hip joint, where it was bound by the girdle he had worn yesterday. Everything was in place. If he could remain immobilized for another day or two, he would be walking in a week. But they expected Esau to come today.

She smiled brightly down on her husband. "Today is a big day, Israel. Your brother is coming to visit. It should be exciting!"

"I know. It will be . . . good to see him again."

He reached for her, and she felt his hand grasping hers. An unspoken understanding flowed between them. Something had happened yesterday, something momentous. In the darkness of that early morning, God had touched their lives. They both knew this had turned everything around. Somehow it was symbolized in Jacob's new name, which both of them accepted. And this acceptance was an unspoken bond between them.

Esau arrived in Mahanaim in midafternoon. By then, Jacob was ready for him. Preparations during the day had been frantic, but through it all Jacob and Leah had laughed away the fears of Rachel, the servants, and all Jacob's sons. Their optimism and cheerfulness were infectious, and soon all the camp was looking forward to Esau's coming.

Jacob met him at the edge of camp. They had rigged a seat for him, a cross between a litter and a chair. Two posts had been set up with a crossbar at the top. The chair-litter was suspended between them. Jacob was comfortable but couldn't move.

Behind him, in a semicircle, ranged his family. Closest to him was Rachel, holding the baby, Joseph, in her arms. Then Leah, holding the child Dinah, with her six boys behind her. On each end of the semicircle were the two maidservants, each with their two children.

Leah wondered how it would look to Esau: a defenseless group, with women and babies, small boys, and a crippled man in the center. How would Esau react to this peaceful scene?

As Esau and his warriors approached, the family grew quiet, their cheerful composure challenged by the warlike appearance of the small army approaching. Leah wondered how many men were with Esau. Twenty would be enough.

Only Jacob and Leah retained their confidence. Leah sensed the chilly tenseness of the others; this might well be their last few moments of life.

Leah wished she could see Esau. But from long practice she had learned to picture in her mind the scene, and she did that now: a fierce, huge man, heavily bearded, his red hair shaggy. He carried a bow, the weapon of a hunter. He was strong enough to annihilate Jacob's family by himself, without the help of the band of armed men behind him.

Leah's confidence began to waver, and she whispered softly into the stillness, "Israel." Perhaps if she reminded herself of the new name, she would regain her courage.

"*Jacob*!" The harsh voice roared from about thirty paces away. "*My brother*!" His feet pounded on the ground as he ran forward.

Leah reached out to Reuben, standing next to her. "What's happening?" she asked urgently.

Reuben answered with a brief laugh, "He's embracing Father! What a fierce bear hug!"

Again Leah pictured the scene: the red-bearded giant bending over to enfold Jacob, who squirmed in the sling. She heard her husband grunt. Would it dislodge the bone from its socket?

"It's good to see you again, brother," said Jacob. "Your greeting shakes me to the bones!"

Esau laughed, loud and long. "I hope my enthusiasm hasn't hurt you much. Your servant Omri told me about your accident. Is it serious?"

"No. A dislocated bone, that's all. In a few days I'll be walking. And are you well?"

"Well enough." Esau's manner was bluff. Abruptly he jerked around to stare at the semicircle of Jacob's family. "And who are these people?"

"My family." Jacob called them forward one at a time and introduced them.

"I count two wives, two concubines, eleven boys, and one girl," said Esau with a laugh. "You've been busy these past twenty years, brother!"

"God has blessed me."

"And what about those flocks and herds I met as I came? Are they yours too?"

"No, Esau. They're yours. They're my gift to you."

"You're very kind, Jacob. But I don't need them. I have plenty. Keep what you have."

"Please accept them," said Jacob. "They're my gift to you. They express my gratitude to see your . . . er, smiling face."

Esau's laugh was loud and hearty. "My *smiling* face! You thought it would be my frowning face, didn't you?" And again he laughed, so that Jacob had no need to answer.

Abruptly Esau turned serious. "Come home with me, Jacob," he said. "My men and I will accompany you to the land of Seir, where you shall be my guests as long as you want to stay."

Leah tensed when she heard the invitation. Would Jacob have enough sense to refuse it? He knew the volatile nature of his unpredictable brother. Too close an association would bring on quarrels, and Esau's hearty good humor could turn into violent bursts of temper.

Jacob chuckled. "Thanks for the invitation, brother. But as you can see, some of the children are small, and the flocks and herds have their young. If they're driven too hard, they'll die. You go on ahead. We'll follow at our own pace."

Leah nodded thoughtfully. Jacob wasn't saying no, but he wasn't saying yes, either.

"Well," said Esau, "at least let me leave you some of my men to assist you and be your guides."

"That won't be necessary, brother, but thank you for your kindness. We'll get along just fine."

"All right, Jacob. Then I'll say good-bye for now."

Again Leah heard Jacob's grunt and knew he was

trying to survive another embrace. A final good-bye, and Esau turned and strode off with his men. The whole interview had taken just a few minutes, but it was enough. Esau was a man of action. To sit around and make small talk wasn't his style. Chances were good he and Jacob would never meet again.

As Esau and his men walked off into the distance, an audible sigh went up from Jacob's family. They crowded around him.

"We're safe, my darling!" said Rachel, and Leah knew she was showing her dimples in a sparkling smile. "Jacob, you were magnificent! All is well now!" Her embrace wouldn't be as bone-shattering as Esau's.

When Leah came to him, he grabbed her hand. "It went just as we expected, didn't it, Leah?" The firm grip of his hand on hers warmed her.

"Yes, Israel," she said tenderly.

"Please have the servants carry me to Rachel's tent for the night. If Esau's hugs can't dislodge my bones, nothing will."

Leah turned away, quickly, before Jacob could see what was in her eyes. "Yes, Israel," she murmured, and hurried off to call the servants.

The sun was sinking over the hills as Leah sat in front of her tent. Alone. Jacob had gone with Rachel to spend the night with her. Leah was glad it was a mile away. She didn't want to hear the giggles, the soft murmurs, the occasional burst of laughter she knew would be coming from Rachel's tent.

She smiled to herself as an evening breeze blew against her forehead. She had long ago accepted her role in her husband's household. She knew what her place was. And it was good. Not even the burden of Reuben's loss of the birthright troubled her tonight.

Soon, they would go home—their new home: the

land of Canaan, Israel's inheritance. Leah, perhaps even more than her husband, understood what this inheritance was, and how Esau's acquiescence guaranteed it. Israel now had eleven sons, and the birthright would be passed to them. They would be the inheritors of the Promise: that through them and their descendants, all the people of the world would be blessed.

"Good night, Israel," she whispered into the evening breeze.

12

Jacob never saw Esau again. Keeping a good distance between the brothers was the best recipe for peace and brotherly love. But Jacob kept in touch with Esau and learned of his growing family and wealth. The livestock Jacob had given him had made Esau the wealthiest man in Seir.

Jacob led his clan across the Jordan River and settled, at least temporarily, near Shechem. His original intent was to migrate eventually to Beersheba, where his father, Isaac, had lived so many years. But for now they lived in the northern part of the land of Canaan.

The people of the land were hospitable—or perhaps a little afraid of this wealthy clan. The boys as they grew to manhood displayed a warlike appearance. Leah felt she was losing control of them. They had once turned to her for counsel, especially Reuben, but now they were increasingly independent, making decisions about pasturing and breeding without consulting even their father.

One day, when the boys were scattered with the flocks, Jacob came to Leah's tent.

"Good morning, Leah." His voice was as cheerful and vibrant as ever, but the gray in his hair and beard were signs of his decreasing vigor. He stayed in the tents now more often than he went to the fields.

"Ah, Israel." Leah continued to call him that, even though she was the only one. Perhaps no one but she realized the significance of the name. "And where is your favorite son today?"

"I sent him to the field with a message for Judah. He should be back tomorrow."

It was strange, how Jacob looked to his fourth son for leadership these days. Yet not so strange, decided Leah. His brothers often turned to him. Reuben was too soft-hearted, and Simeon and Levi too temperamental. Only Judah had the qualities these fierce young men would respect and follow.

Leah frowned. "You must speak to Joseph, Israel. Even if he is your favorite, he mustn't brag about it in front of his brothers."

Jacob squatted on the carpet beside Leah. "Don't worry about Joseph. Nobody will harm him. Everybody knows he's the favorite."

"But our sons are so fierce! Who knows what they'll do?"

"You're right about that." Jacob pulled on his gray beard. "Just yesterday they killed a servant of the Hivites for moving a few sheep into the water hole ahead of their own."

"Oh. Trouble. What happened after that?"

Jacob grinned. "Judah sent a gift to Hamor the Hivite in Shechem. Four camels—one male and three females. That should ensure peace. But I don't think anybody around here wants to start trouble. Not with *our* boys."

Leah shook her head. "The trouble, if it comes, won't come from the Hivites. It will come from our sons. Especially Simeon and Levi. You know what they're like."

Jacob nodded slowly. "Yes. But I think I have the answer to that."

"Oh? What is it?"

"The son of Hamor the Hivite—his name is Shechem, just like their city—needs a wife. Why don't we marry our daughter to him?"

"Yes, that should be a good match—if Dinah is agreeable."

Jacob snorted. "We'll do it whether she's agreeable or not! She's no use to us as she is. And besides, this young man Shechem is a good-looking boy, and his father's wealthy. He calls himself king of the Hivites. Huh! He doesn't even know what a real king is!"

Leah lowered her eyes and stared at the carpet she sat on. With her husband's attitude, Dinah would have no say in whom she married. But she *did* have to marry someday—soon. She was several years past marriageable age. Before long no one would accept her as bride.

Jacob glanced around. "Where is Dinah today?"

"I don't know. She left early this morning. Sometimes she goes out for the whole day. I don't know where she goes."

"Oh. Well, when you see her, tell her about our plans. Meanwhile, I'll go over to Shechem myself and talk to this 'king.' " The word was a sneer. "Maybe I can arrange a suitable bride-price."

Jacob stood slowly, obviously finding it more and more difficult to do even such small tasks as standing after he had been sitting awhile.

"I think," he said as he walked toward the door of the tent, "we should marry our daughter to this boy within the next month. Yes. It might prevent trouble between our sons and the Hivites."

Leah spent a restless night waiting for Dinah. She didn't return. That wasn't like Dinah. She was often gone a whole day but had always returned by nightfall.

In the morning she sent her maid Zilpah to find Jacob and tell him of Dinah's disappearance. She returned a few minutes later with the message that Jacob had gone yesterday to the city of Shechem and would return today. He was obviously wasting no time finding a husband for his daughter.

Neither Jacob nor Dinah returned to Leah's tent that day, but she wasn't worried. They were undoubtedly together, and negotiations were being conducted for a bride-price.

The next morning, Jacob returned—alone.

Leah was sitting on the mat just outside the tent in the cool of morning, enjoying the sunshine. The concern in her husband's voice startled her.

"What is it, Israel? Where's Dinah?"

"She's—well, she's at Shechem." He sat on the mat beside her.

"Shechem? Why?"

"She's—she's already married to that boy."

"What?"

Jacob sighed. "Yes. I made it official yesterday. I placed her hand in the hand of Shechem in the presence of his father, Hamor. I certified her virginity. But when I did, Hamor laughed. Evidently Dinah and Shechem have been seeing each other for a long time."

"Oh!" Leah felt a cold chill inside her. How could it have happened? She and Dinah were so close. So intimate. She knew all her daughter's secrets. No confidence had been withheld from her. Leah shook her head and bit her lip. Tears welled in her eyes.

Jacob took her hand. "Leah, don't blame yourself. Dinah has been sneaking out to meet with the young man for months, without our knowledge. We're well rid of her."

"Israel, how can you say that? Our daughter—"

Jacob snorted. "Our daughter has been rutting

113

around, acting like a Canaanite. She's no better than they. Maybe that boy will take a stick to her, like all those Hivite men do to their women. She should have had that a long time ago."

"Israel, please!" Leah's voice was a whisper. She shivered, feeling the tears running down her cheeks.

Suddenly, Jacob's hand tightened on hers, and his voice grew softer. "I'm sorry, Leah. I didn't mean to hurt you. I know how much Dinah meant to you. But maybe it's all for the best."

"Do our other sons know?"

"Yes. I met Simeon and Levi on the way home and told them. They'll tell the others. I also asked them to send Joseph back to the tents. I don't like him out in the field, even if he is ten—"

"Simeon and Levi!" Leah looked up at him sharply. "Oh, Israel, please, go out to the field immediately and find our sons! You know what they're like! Please!"

"It's all right, Leah. They won't—" He looked closely at her. "All right. I'll go if you want me to. But—"

"Please hurry! It may already be too late!"

Jacob didn't return to the cluster of tents in the valley by the stream that day. Nor the next. On the third day, Joseph returned—alone.

"Mother Leah!" The boy burst into Leah's tent as she sat on the carpet. The black curly hair above the round cherubic face was tangled and sweaty.

"What is it, boy?"

"Father says to tell you everything's all right now. They reached an agreement with the Hivites at Shechem. They're all going to be circumcised!"

Leah gasped. "Circumcised! How do you know?"

Joseph flopped down on the carpet beside her, close enough for her to see his face. The boy was grinning. He had two dimples on his cheeks, just like his mother's.

"Well, Simeon and Levi came back to our camp and told us about Dinah's marriage. They called it 'rape' and wanted to attack those Hivites and kill 'em all. But Reuben said no, Father wouldn't approve. So Judah came up with an idea. He and Reuben went to Shechem and made a deal with those funny Hivites. They could marry one of us only if all of them became circumcised. So they did. Right then and there! By the time Father arrived in our camp, it was all done. What do you think of that?"

Leah breathed easier. Circumcision! Reuben and Judah had turned aside the quick temper of their hotheaded brothers by this clever scheme. The Hivites had now become followers of their God. It wouldn't matter to these superstitious Canaanites what god they followed, but to the sons of Israel, that was important. By becoming members of their own faith, they had turned aside any thoughts of vengeance and made possible peace between the two clans.

"Thank you, Joseph. You've brought me good news." She put her hand on his arm. "Have you told your mother yet?"

"No. I came straight here, because I knew you wanted to know."

She smiled at him. "How thoughtful. Now go to your mother. Rachel will be glad to see you."

"Aw, Mother always worries about me. I don't know why she should. I'm God's favorite as well as Father's."

The boy rose and ran out of the tent.

Leah sighed. Joseph! The boy was lovable, even if he was arrogant. She smiled. At least he had accepted Jacob's God, rather than Rachel's teraphim. But Leah herself was partly responsible for that, for she had spent much time with him during the past few years. Jacob hadn't allowed him to go to the fields at age five as the other boys had, so Joseph was often in Leah's tent. Many times Leah had gone on long walks with him, holding his sleeve and letting him be her eyes, while she had talked about the great and good God they followed.

Joseph was intelligent and personable, and Leah had no trouble keeping her promise to herself, that she would accept and love the favorite son—the birthright boy—as much as her other sons. And he would become even closer to her, she hoped, now that Dinah was gone.

Dinah—gone!

For the first time, the reality fully pierced her. She had worried before, then felt relief at Joseph's news about the circumcision of the Hivites. Now the full impact of what had happened struck her. She was alone! Gone forever was her beautiful daughter! So cheerful, so loving, so companionable! Alone.

No. Not alone. She still had Joseph. But he would soon go to the field. Then truly she would be alone.

But she still had Israel. She would always have Israel. Even if she had to share him with Rachel.

She smiled. Even that thought had become more bearable with the years. Especially now. Israel was growing older, and his sexual vigor was diminishing. He still spent his nights in Rachel's tents, but more and more he spent his days with Leah. The companionship they shared during these years was ever more pleasant and warm. Growing old, she told herself, wasn't too much of a burden—if you had someone to grow old with!

The next morning, Joseph came to Leah's tent for an early walk. Taking Leah's hand, he led her to the stream. This wasn't the first time he had done this, and Leah treasured these times together almost as much as her walks with Jacob. Joseph evidently enjoyed them also.

Soon they would need to go back to the tent. This was the dry season, and the hot sun would burn Leah's sensitive skin if she stayed out too long. She breathed deeply of the dusty air, smelling the moisture of the stream. She listened to the croak of the frogs and their splashes as they dove into the water to escape the two invading humans.

Leah always enjoyed Joseph's laughter, and he was now entertaining her with a story about the frogs they had chased into the muddy bottom of the stream. But she turned serious as she realized the direction his funny story was leading.

"And then this one little frog, he sat on the bank and the sun shone on him. And all the other frogs—all ten of them—looked at him and bowed down to him. Because he was the best frog in the whole stream!"

"Joseph!" Her tone was sharp—sharper than she intended. But it caught his attention.

"Yes, Mother Leah? What's wrong?"

She paused, frowning. How should she say it? "Joseph, listen to me. I know exactly what you're saying. You mustn't say things like that. Not to me, not to your mother and father, and especially not to your brothers!"

"Aw, why not, Mother Leah? It's true, isn't it?"

She caught her breath. They had been over this before. The boy firmly believed it. As the favorite son, he would some day rule his ten brothers.

"Whether it's true or not, you mustn't say it. Don't you know what that kind of talk does to your brothers? They're jealous of you. They might hurt you—"

"Don't worry about me, Mother. God is with me. After all, I'm the heir of the Promise. If God took care of

117

Father all those years, with Esau and Laban and all the other troubles he had, God'll take care of me too."

"But, Joseph—"

She stopped as she heard the crunch of sandals on the path. Jacob's. He was home, then. But why? Was something wrong?

"It's Father!" Joseph pressed her hand. "He's back!"

"Leah!"

By his voice, Leah knew there was trouble. She stepped toward him, holding out her hands.

"Joseph," he said solemnly. "Go back to the tents. I want to talk to Leah alone."

"All right, Father." The boy sounded puzzled, but he obeyed. His footsteps pounded away toward the tents.

"What is it, Israel? Trouble?"

Jacob didn't answer at first. He held both her hands. His forehead was creased in a frown.

When he spoke, it was with a tremor. "Leah. Something dreadful has happened!"

"What?"

He struggled to find the words. "Simeon and Levi . . . you know how they felt about those Hivites in Shechem. Well, they slaughtered them!"

"No! All of them?"

"Just the men."

"And . . . Dinah?"

"They took her away. I don't know where. They plundered the city, took everything of value, burned the rest, and sold the women and children into slavery. They've made us look like monsters to all the people in the land of Canaan!"

"But—I don't believe it! How could such a thing happen?"

Jacob took a deep breath. "The Hivites all agreed to circumcision. The whole town. They did it. And while

118

they were recovering, Simeon and Levi came during the night and killed the men in the town."

"But Dinah? Where is she?"

"I don't know. I just don't know. Oh, Leah, I'm so sorry!"

"No!" Leah threw herself into Jacob's arms. "No! No! No!" She sobbed into his chest.

His arms tightened around her. No words were said. But somehow, he gave her his strength. His arms around her were what she needed now. He must never let her go. Never. Never.

And he didn't. He held her in silence as the sun mounted. The heat surged into her, burning the back of her head. And still he held her, strongly, silently, giving himself and his strength to her.

When at last he led her back to the coolness of the tent, she had mastered herself. Her daughter was gone. Her sons were disinherited. The boy Joseph, Rachel's son, was the heir of the Promise. And Rachel was her husband's favorite wife.

But she still had him. Or at least a part of him. The part of him that she needed. That gave her strength. And courage to face the days ahead.

13

Leah never learned Dinah's fate. Levi and Simeon refused to tell her. From what they said, Leah suspected Dinah had taken her own life. But her sons would neither confirm nor deny this.

Following the slaughter of the Hivites in Shechem, Jacob decided to move on. The Perizzites, who lived in the area, began to fortify some of their cities. Whether this meant they were preparing to attack Jacob's clan, or merely afraid of an attack by the warlike sons of Israel, Jacob didn't bother to find out. Anyway, he told Leah, he wanted to push farther south, eventually migrating to Beersheba, where he would settle permanently.

But first, he went to the small Canaanite town of Luz and pitched his tents about a mile west of the settlement in a rocky valley.

"Why here?" asked Judah. "There's barely enough water to support our people, let alone the livestock. We'll have to range far to the south to find pasture."

"I know," replied Jacob. "I'm stopping here because this place holds precious memories for me. You and your brothers may push on with the livestock, and we'll catch up with you near Ephrath."

Judah's deep voice was quiet and confident. "We'll start immediately, before our herds muddy the water."

"No." Jacob paused. "Start tomorrow. Today, let's build an altar here and offer a sacrifice as my father, Isaac, used to do."

This puzzled Judah, but not Leah. She knew from what Jacob had told her that this was where he had had his first encounter with the God he served. Many years ago, while fleeing his brother, Jacob had stopped here and dreamed of a ladder, and of God at the top of the ladder. The vision had assured him of the Promise that through Jacob and his descendants all the world would be blessed.

Jacob led them to a stone he had set on end many years ago to commemorate the place. It was on a rocky hillside overlooking the valley and its small stream. It looked like a giant hand had upended the rock. Surely Jacob hadn't done it himself! Yet he claimed he had.

Jacob asked each of his sons to select a perfect beast from among the livestock for the sacrifice. Soon they drove to the altar a variety of animals: bullocks, rams, he-goats, even one camel. Jacob inspected each and declared it perfect, free of blemish, fit for sacrifice to God.

He stood before the huge stone, knife in hand, a warm breeze blowing his long, gray beard and hair. Around him were gathered all the people in the clan: his sons, wives, concubines, servants, herdsmen. All were quiet. The only sounds came from the animals, bleating and baaing and mooing as though they knew what was to happen.

Jacob had laid a large pit fire in a cleft of rock near the altar. Leah caught a faint whiff of smoke in the air.

Jacob spoke then, and his strong voice reached out into the valley.

"This is truly the house of God, God's dwelling-place. I am Israel, he who wrestles with God. And here in this holy place, I renew my covenant with the God of my fathers, Abraham and Isaac, for God has given this land to me and my descendants. Through us, all people on earth will be blessed!"

As Leah listened, she realized the effect these words had on Jacob's sons. She wondered if Reuben, standing beside his massive bullock, believed that he, as oldest son, would get this birthright and the Promise which went with it. Perhaps Judah wondered that also, since he was gradually taking over the leadership of the clan. And Joseph. He would be smiling now, believing that the Promise would be his someday.

But Jacob wasn't finished. "Let everyone who has not given his total allegiance to our God do so now. During the next few days, bring to this place all idols, whether wooden or gold, and bury them there, under that tree."

He pointed to a large oak tree below. Its gnarled trunk and drooping boughs looked stately and dignified, as though it were proclaiming itself guardian of this valley.

Why had Jacob made this request now? Leah frowned. Did he suspect that some of the servants and herdsmen from Haran still held onto their household gods? He had made it clear from the beginning that their circumcision meant instant acceptance into his faith. Did he suspect that his own beloved wife—Joseph's mother—still clung to her teraphim?

"Reuben." Jacob's resonant voice rose and reverberated in the rocky valley. "Bring the first sacrifice."

For once in her life, Leah was glad she couldn't see the ceremony. She heard the shouts of the men, the shrieks—yes, shrieks!—of the livestock, their death throes, and behind her, the gasps and sobs of the women and servants as they watched this grisly ritual.

Leah pulled the cowl of her burnoose around her head to protect her from the sun. The ceremony seemed to take forever. Soon Leah began to smell a different odor—burning flesh. Sacrifices offered to the living God. She wondered about this part of the ritual. Was God feasting on the proffered meat? That was ridiculous. What was the purpose of sacrifice, anyway?

Tradition. That had to be it. Something begun by Abraham, passed on to Isaac, and continued now with Israel and his sons. There was value in tradition, since it was a tangible ceremony binding the generations together and unifying their faith.

Symbolism, too. Leah tugged her ear as a new thought struck her. Some religions she had heard about offered human sacrifices—even a son or daughter—in the absurd belief that the more valued the sacrifice, the greater impression it would have on the god. But Jacob's clan had never done that. Why? Was it because this was a symbolic substitute? She decided she would ask Jacob about this some time.

The ceremony lasted well into the evening, and Leah was exhausted. The sun had sapped her energy, and she gladly retired to her tent.

The next day, during the confusion and bustle of the departure of the herds and flocks, she sought out her sister.

"Rachel," she called from the door of the tent.

Rachel appeared at the door, wide-eyed. "How did you get here, Leah? Isn't it dangerous to wander around with all that's happening? You could have been trampled!"

"Zilpah brought me. No bull would dare attack her!"

Rachel laughed. Although she was too far away for Leah to see her, her dimples undoubtedly added charm and vitality to an already perfect face. Even in her forties, after giving birth to a child, Rachel retained the slimness and beauty of youth. And youth's bubbling personality.

"Wasn't that a perfectly horrid ceremony yesterday? All that blood! You should have seen Jacob's clothes last night. They were filthy! And everything stinks today. Making a sacrifice just doesn't smell the same as cooking food."

Leah smiled as Rachel led her to the carpet, where she settled as comfortably as she could. She accepted the wine cup Rachel thrust into her hand, but she didn't drink. Wine in the morning unsettled her stomach.

Rachel prattled on, talking about Joseph and the fine camel he had chosen for a sacrifice. "Our best one," she pouted. "Gentle for riding. I tried to talk him into using that miserable old male that tried to bite me last week. But Joseph insisted it had to be the best, and Jacob said it was a perfect choice. It does seem such a shame—"

"Rachel." Leah knew the only way to say what she came here to say was to interrupt the shallow monologue.

"What is it, dear sister?"

"The part of the ritual I liked was when he called on all of us to rededicate ourselves to our faith in God."

She paused, and was instantly aware of Rachel's silence. But she had to continue.

"Please, Rachel. Do as he said. Bury the teraphim under the oak tree!"

Again the tense silence. When Rachel finally spoke, her voice was a whisper. "You haven't told him, have you?"

"No. I promised I wouldn't. But if he finds out—"

"He won't. Not unless you tell him. Please, Leah. I

need my gods. I can't accept your bloody God whom I can't see or understand. Please don't let Jacob take the teraphim from me!"

"Rachel—"

Suddenly Rachel was on her knees beside Leah, her arms around her shoulders. There were tears in her eyes.

"Please, dear sister! Let me have my teraphim! It's all I have left of home!"

"Home! But this is your home! With your husband, your son! The place doesn't matter. People do. There's nothing back in Haran but our father, and neither of us misses *him* too much."

"You don't understand!" Rachel's voice was a sob. "My teraphim help me! Without them, I'm . . . I'm nothing. Nobody. If it weren't for them, I wouldn't have Joseph, or Jacob's love, or anything!"

"I do understand." Leah tried to make her voice as gentle as possible. Her arms went around Rachel, and she held her tightly.

Leah understood perfectly. It was still a contest, between the invisible God and the strength of the idols concealed somewhere in Rachel's tent. To Rachel's way of thinking, they were evenly matched. Jacob's God had increased his wealth, won him the battle of wits with Laban, and delivered Jacob from the hand of Esau. Then this God had given Jacob many sons.

Rachel believed the teraphim had given her the two things she wanted most: Jacob's love and the favorite son. But Leah knew that Rachel didn't understand the true significance of either gift.

She saw Jacob's love as the physical attraction which brought him to her tent every night. This, to Rachel, was what love was all about. Nothing more. She believed she had *all* Jacob's love.

125

Also, to Rachel, the favorite son meant only that Jacob loved Joseph above all his other sons. Nothing more. She had no grasp of the meaning of the phrase "heir to the Promise." To her, birthright meant simply that the favorite son would gain the largest portion of Jacob's wealth at his death. Her son, Joseph, would carry on the tradition of the tribe: Abraham, Isaac, Jacob—and Joseph.

Two things her teraphim had given her: Jacob's love and the favorite son. Her gods were therefore equal to Leah's God.

And something more. Leah, with sudden insight, knew that her shallow sister would never understand about Jacob and his God, no matter how patiently she explained it to her. Rachel would neither understand nor accept. And by forcing Rachel to give up her idols and embrace an incomprehensible God, Leah would not only confuse and embitter her sister but gain her hatred.

"It's all right, Rachel," she whispered. "Keep your teraphim. I'll not tell our husband."

"Oh, thank you, dear, dear sister!" Rachel's tear-stained eyes looked into Leah's. "You don't know how much this means to me!"

"I do know," replied Leah. And to herself she added, *I understand more than you do*!

14

The next day, a messenger arrived from the Canaanite town of Luz, just a mile to the east. Jacob received
him joyfully. He brought news of an old family servant
living in Luz, who wanted Jacob to visit her.

Leah went with him. She rode an ass while Jacob
walked. Her sons had gone south with the livestock,
but Joseph had stayed behind. He, too, accompanied
them.

On the way, Jacob explained to Leah that the old
lady who requested this visit was his mother's child-
hood nurse and lifelong companion. Leah looked forward to meeting her.

In Luz, the messenger took them to a small house in
the center of the town. Only about fifty people lived
here, Leah decided. They weren't prosperous. The
houses were mere hovels with mud walls and thatched
roofs. The children were naked and their parents were
in rags. They all seemed to shrink into their sloven
huts as though fearful of the leader of the fierce clan
which had invaded their peaceful area.

The house the messenger led them to was about the
same size as the others, but better kept. The area
around the house had been swept. Inside there was a
carpet to sit on. Jacob preceded his wife and son as he
entered the house.

"Deborah!" He shouted, and ran forward.

In the darkness of the interior, Leah could see nothing of the person her husband embraced. But she heard her wheezing, and suspected she was old. She seemed to be having trouble speaking. Was she dumb?

Jacob helped Deborah sit on the carpet, then motioned his wife and son to join him. Leah chose to sit as near as possible to their ancient hostess. She wanted to see her face.

It was old. Very old. The wrinkles and wispy white hair and toothless mouth spoke of more than years. Leah saw in that face something she hadn't seen before but recognized instantly: wisdom.

The messenger had told them Deborah was a witch. The people of Luz called upon her often as a midwife. They respected her for her lore of herbs and healing potions. But they feared her, too. They thought she healed people by magic.

As Leah looked into her face, the old lady bobbed her head and sniffed.

"Le-Leah," she said.

Leah wasn't surprised she knew her name. News traveled fast. Everyone in Luz would know by now all about Jacob and his family. Even the details.

The old lady then turned her gaze on the boy.

"J-Joseph." She bobbed her head. "B-b-born to b-be a king!"

Joseph laughed. "That's right, Grandmother. How did you know?"

But Deborah just sniffed and said nothing.

Jacob found it difficult to get his hostess to talk. He plied her with questions, to which she either nodded, shook her head, or gave one-word answers. Evidently her stammering made her self-conscious, and she said as little as possible.

128

"My mother used to tell me," said Jacob, "that you correctly predicted twins before my brother and I were born. Is that really true?"

Deborah winked and nodded.

"And did you really say that we sounded inside her body like 'two nations warring'?" Again the nod. "Well, you were right—at least in part. But no more. Esau and I have made up our differences. We live in peace now."

The old lady frowned. The wrinkles on her forehead jumped around above her eyes.

"S-s-still at w-w-war!" she muttered.

"No, no. You're wrong. We met last year at Mahanaim beyond the Jordan River. We parted friends. No more wars."

Deborah sniffed. But she said nothing. She didn't need to. She had already said it.

Leah felt a chill. The townspeople had called her a witch. They were close. But what they had called witchcraft was really intelligence and wisdom. Did she know something about Esau? And about Joseph?

"Grandmother," she said softly, "do you think all will be well with Israel?"

Deborah turned toward her, her eyes wide and questioning.

"Is-Is-Israel?" She bobbed her head and winked. As she looked at Leah, her eyes seemed to penetrate deeply inside her. Then she sniffed. "You. B-b-best wife!"

Jacob laughed. "No, Deborah. Wrong again. My 'best' wife is Rachel. She's the mother of Joseph here. The one who's 'born to be a king'!"

Deborah turned toward Jacob, and her eyes were scornful. Then she turned to Joseph, who was staring at her in awe.

"T-trouble!" she muttered.

Jacob asked her what she meant, but Deborah wouldn't reply. Perhaps she felt she had said enough. Leah stared at the old lady until her eyes blurred. How much did she really know of the future? Was she accurate in all she had said?

Then suddenly the old lady turned to Jacob and blurted, "B-b-bury me at B-b-bethel!"

"Bethel?" Jacob shook his head. " 'God's house?' Where's that?"

But the old lady had shut her mouth and would say no more. Soon Jacob and his family took their leave. Deborah kissed each one but said nothing.

As they left the house and made their way through the small village to take the path for home, Leah wondered about what she had heard today. Predictions of the future? Shrewd guesses? Or just the babblings of an addled old lady?

Deborah wanted to be buried at Bethel. Did she mean the altar where the sacrifices had been offered two days ago? Jacob had called it that during the ceremony, but how could she know that?

Esau, she had said, was still at war with Jacob. Could they expect trouble from him in the future? Or was she referring to future generations?

And Joseph—*born to be a king*. What did that mean? And that other word: *trouble*. She felt the same chill inside her she felt a few moments ago in Deborah's house. What lay ahead for young Joseph?

Leah had been surprised at Deborah's reaction to Jacob's new name. At first, Deborah had shown surprise at his being called "Israel." But then she had nodded. Deborah had understood. That was more believable. Deborah in her wisdom would know that Jacob was one who "wrestled with God."

And finally, Leah worked around in her mind the utterly incredible statement about her being Jacob's "best wife." That was impossible. Jacob was right: Rachel was the "best wife." Leah had long ago accepted that.

But what if the old woman really knew what she was talking about?

Only a week after their visit to Deborah in Luz, the same messenger brought word that Deborah had died. Her dying request was that she be buried in "Bethel."

Jacob went immediately to Luz. He returned the same day with Deborah's body. He buried her under the oak tree in the valley of Bethel, as Jacob now insisted the place be called. This was the first grave under the "Weeping Oak."

The next day, Jacob led Leah at dawn to the grave. They stood under the old oak and stared at the site.

"The last of the old ones," said Jacob.

Leah shook her head. "Not so, Israel. Now *we* are the old ones."

Jacob nodded, running his fingers through his gray beard. "And perhaps the next to die?" he muttered.

"Do you fear death?"

"No." Jacob spoke softly but confidently. "Not since I wrestled with God at the fords of Jabbok. My life— and my death—are in God's hands. I'm content."

"You've found peace, then, Israel."

"Let's say I'm not wrestling as hard as I once did. I suppose you could call that peace."

It felt right to stand at Deborah's grave and talk about dying. Death seemed so natural, so expected. As they turned to leave, Leah clutched Jacob's sleeve and whispered, "I'm content, too, Israel. If I died tomorrow, it would be all right. I too have found peace."

He smiled and pressed her hand. "If only Rachel would feel as you do," he murmured.

15

They spent five years at Bethel. It wasn't a good place for the livestock. Jacob's sons scattered and ranged far afield in their search for pasture and water. Jacob still wouldn't let Joseph go to the field to work as a herdsman. The young man showed a talent for bookkeeping, and his tallies of the growing herds and flocks were accurate.

Joseph's work often took him to the field for a day to take a new count of the livestock. As his excursions took him further and further away from home, and he often spent two or three nights away, Rachel fretted.

"What if a wild animal caught him in the wilderness?" she asked Leah one day. "Would he stand a chance by himself?"

"Don't worry about him, Rachel." Leah placed a comforting hand on her sister's arm. "He's a man now. A strong man. We can't shield him from trouble forever."

Leah worried more about her sons harming Joseph rather than wild animals. She was well aware of their jealousy, which they now proclaimed openly. It wasn't just because of Joseph's favorite status. They could have accepted that if only he had been humble about it.

But he wasn't. He bragged about it.

Not only that, but he came to his father occasionally with tales about how "those boys" were doing things that would bring dishonor to Jacob's good name. The brothers' were high-spirited young men who often picked fights with the local inhabitants, or molested their women, or confiscated the best grazing land. And Joseph told all.

But there was more: Joseph's dreams.

Leah heard about these dreams from her sons. Reuben kept her informed about the brothers growing resentment toward Joseph and the dreams he boasted about.

"Mother, something must be done about that boy." Reuben rubbed the back of his hand against his curly brown beard. "It's the *way* he tells us about those dreams that we can't stand."

Leah sighed. "What's his latest dream, Reuben?"

"Just last week he dreamed about a grainfield, already harvested and in sheaves. Then, in his dream, one sheaf stood upright, and the others—ten of them—bowed down before it. He left us little doubt about its meaning."

Leah bit her lip. This wasn't the first time. The dreams themselves didn't shock her. They might even be accurate predictors of the future. What bothered her was the way he flaunted it before his brothers.

"Try to be patient, son," she said. "He's young. Perhaps a little maturity—"

"He'd better hurry and grow up!" Reuben snapped. "If this keeps up, he might not get much older!"

Leah could well believe it. If Reuben, the kindest and gentlest of the brothers, was upset and losing patience, how much more must the others be? She would speak to Rachel about it.

But Rachel turned a deaf ear, saying those boys

would never harm Jacob's favorite. Next Leah turned to Jacob.

Jacob had come again from Rachel's tent in the early morning. Sometimes they went to the Weeping Oak and stood by Deborah's grave. Sometimes they climbed the hillside to the altar of sacrifice. This morning they walked along the stream running through the little valley.

Leah was uncertain how to begin, but she knew she must. "We have a family problem, Israel." She clung to his sleeve as they threaded their way through the rocks along the path.

"Family problem? With eleven healthy sons? And Joseph at sixteen showing signs of being an exceptional manager of the business? And you tell me we have a family problem!" He chuckled. "It must be gigantic!"

"It is, and it's serious." She tried to keep her voice from showing the irritation she felt at his flippancy. "It's Joseph. His brothers hate him and may harm him."

"But they know he's the favorite."

"Favorite he may be, but that won't protect him from his brothers. You know how they are. Simeon especially. He's the most outspoken against Joseph. All the boys hate him. Even Reuben."

"Reuben? Gentle Reuben? Well, no matter. Judah will keep the boys in line."

"But Judah is beginning to hate Joseph, too."

She looked up at Jacob, who frowned as he saw her face.

"Don't worry, Leah. I think I know how to solve the problem."

Leah relaxed a little. "I knew you'd think of a way. Tell me about it, Israel."

"What those boys need is a reminder that Joseph is

the favorite. The heir of the Promise. Protected by God as well as by me. I think I know how to do that."

"How?"

"I shall give him a new robe." Jacob grinned. "It shall be a robe clearly marking him as the favorite. The sleeves will be long, and the hem will reach the ground. It shall be made of good-quality linen purchased from Egypt. But the color is the most important: purple. The color of royalty. And gold. There must be some gold lace woven among the purple."

"And that's all?" Leah was suddenly tense again.

"Of course. When the boys see him in the favorite's robe, they'll remember who he is. They won't dare harm him then."

She shook her head. "You know best, Israel. But I think it would be much more effective if you would talk to him and ask him not to flaunt his favoritism so much before them. And tell him not to brag about his dreams. It irritates his brothers and might push them too far."

"I've heard about his dreams." They paused in the shade of a tree, and Jacob helped Leah sit on one of its roots. The day was beginning to grow hot; soon they would have to return to the tent. "But don't worry about those dreams, Leah. They're simply childish fantasies. He would like to lord it over his brothers. But he'll grow out of it. Think of it as a stage he's passing through."

"But will he pass through it before his brothers' jealousy turns violent?"

"Violence? To the favorite? That's why he'll be wearing the special robe. To remind them."

"I'm not so sure."

"Leah, you've told me often enough, he's the heir to the Promise. God won't let *anything* happen to him!"

There wasn't much more to say. A pious statement like that always seemed to shut down rational discussion. But as Leah bent to wash her face in the cool stream, she was afraid. Her husband thought the robe would prevent violence. She wasn't so sure. It might do just the opposite.

Later that day, Leah had another opportunity to talk with Rachel, but her sister was unable to appreciate her fears. On the contrary, Rachel was delighted with Jacob's plan to give Joseph a fancy new robe.

"It will show his brothers who's the favorite," she said smugly. "Those boys are like animals." Suddenly her forehead creased in a frown. "But it's the other kind of wild animals I'm more concerned about."

The robe was striking. The Egyptian linen, dyed a brilliant Phoenician purple, made it look like the robe of a royal prince. The long sleeves and ground-length hem gave it the regal touch. It sparkled with gold filigree, and had red and green designs along the borders.

Joseph was delighted. "Wait till I show my brothers!" He paraded around the camp, swirling the robe and showing it off to everyone.

Jacob was as proud of it as Joseph was, and would say nothing to the boy about his attitude. Leah felt she at least should try to warn him.

"Joseph, don't brag so much to your brothers. They know you're the favorite. This robe is to remind them. You don't need to keep telling them. Wear it humbly. They will hate you for it otherwise."

But Joseph only grinned. "Don't worry, Mother Leah. This robe isn't the only thing that'll protect me. Remember, I'm the heir to the Promise."

Leah nodded. Joseph, more than his brothers, seemed to grasp the meaning of that phrase. And it was true: God's protection *was* upon the birthright son.

Jacob sent Joseph on a routine errand to the field to find his brothers. The flocks were scattered, seeking water and pasture, and Jacob needed to keep track of them. Joseph was well known to the Canaanites who lived in the area. These natives knew enough about the warlike sons of Jacob to respect the favorite and do him no harm.

As he prepared to leave, Rachel hugged him. "Be careful of wild animals!" she said.

Joseph turned to Leah, who also embraced him. "Be humble to your brothers," she whispered in his ear.

To both warnings, Joseph merely grinned and carelessly waved good-bye.

He didn't come home that night, nor the next. After four days, even Jacob grew anxious.

On the morning of the fifth day, Reuben arrived in camp on a camel which had obviously been ridden hard. He went right to his father. Shortly, Jacob himself mounted a camel, and the two of them set out again. Leah heard all this activity. The feeling that gripped her reminded her of the morning she woke with foreboding on the day of Jacob's injury at the Jabbok River.

Then Rachel came running to Leah's tent.

"Oh, Leah! Leah! Something dreadful has happened!"

"What? Tell me!"

"Reuben says something is wrong with Joseph. I don't know what it is. But it must be something terrible, because Jacob didn't say anything. He just went off with Reuben. Oh, Leah, what is it? What's happened?"

"I don't know, Rachel. We'll just have to wait and see."

They waited three days in mounting terror. As the long days slid by, Leah's fear grew. Something *had* happened; she knew it.

Rachel felt the same. She spent many hours in Leah's tent, wailing and tearing her clothes. She wouldn't eat.

On the afternoon of the third day, Jacob returned. Reuben was with him, and Judah and Simeon. Leah identified them by their voices. They went directly to Rachel's tent.

Then Leah heard Rachel's scream. Leah stumbled out of her tent and groped her way toward the sound of the voices.

Reuben came to her, and his big arm encircled her.

"Tell me, Reuben. What happened to Joseph?"

"Mother, he was attacked by a wild animal, probably a lion. We found his robe."

He led her into Rachel's tent. Her sister was sobbing uncontrollably in Jacob's arms. Judah held the robe.

Leah went to Judah and took the robe from him. It was torn and dirty, and had some ugly brown stains on it.

Leah turned to her sons. "Take me to my tent," she ordered sharply. Reuben and Judah obeyed.

In Leah's tent, she faced her boys. "Tell me the truth! How did this happen?"

"I don't know, Mother." Judah's voice was firm. "We found this in the wilderness. We didn't find the body. But there were signs a lion had been in the area."

"Reuben? I want the truth!"

"Mother, that's all we know."

They were lying. She didn't know why, but she sensed it. She started to say something but stopped herself. It would do no good to accuse these boys. Whatever they had done to Joseph was already done. Nothing could bring him back. It would be better if she never knew what happened. It would be better, too, if Jacob never knew.

"Leah!"

Her husband was calling her. She clutched Reuben's sleeve and walked over to Rachel's tent.

Jacob's voice was urgent. "Can you give Rachel some of that medicine you bought from the Egyptian caravan? She's hysterical."

Leah nodded. Reuben led her back to her tent. There she found the vial with the strange liquid which would relax her sister and make her drowsy. She returned to Rachel's tent and made her drink some. In a few moments, the frantic sobs died out and Rachel slept.

Leah turned to Jacob. "Walk with me, Israel."

They walked down the familiar trail and stood under the Weeping Oak. The rest of the family left them alone, knowing that Leah was what Jacob needed most now. Jacob said nothing, and Leah respected his need for companionship without words.

Leah sensed her husband's silent grief. It hit him now, after leaving Rachel's tent. Back there, he had been concerned with his beloved wife. Now, the magnitude of what had happened struck hard.

Finally he broke the silence.

"My son. My favorite. Leah, what shall I do?"

Leah was ready with an answer. "Have another," she said simply. "Remember his name: Joseph. 'Another.' God will surely give you another son by Rachel."

Jacob shook his head. "I'm old, Leah. I'm not—"

"Children come from God, Israel. Surely God will give you another."

Jacob buried his face in his hands. "I wish it were true. But how can I be sure?"

Leah put her small white hand on his weather-beaten one. "Remember your name: Israel. You're the one who wrestles with God. You know now this means suffering and pain. But put yourself in God's hands. Let God declare your future. Remember, you are Israel!"

Jacob took a deep breath and grasped both her hands. He looked deeply into her eyes. Then he let out his breath with a sigh.

"I wish I had your faith!" he murmured.

Above them, the hot wind rustled the leaves of the old oak tree. Leah looked into her husband's somber face. He would find the burden of Joseph's death greater than Rachel would. Rachel was younger. She would recover quickly.

But Israel? She nodded. Israel would spend his nights in Rachel's tent now. For solace. And because he needed another son. A favorite son. A son to be the heir of the Promise. And Leah would support him even while he slept in that other tent and left her with her tears.

16

As Leah had rightly guessed, Joseph's death was harder for Jacob to accept than for Rachel.

At first, Jacob spent a lot of time alone. He wandered off into the wilderness, sometimes not returning until late evening. After a few weeks, he seemed to accept his grief and was able to talk about it with Leah.

He talked about the destiny of the family and what God had in mind for his descendants. His suffering—his "wrestling with God"—he hoped would be the preparation for a dynasty. Perhaps it was God's will that he, and only he, would suffer. The children of the God-wrestler wouldn't have to endure his anguish.

Rachel recovered from the shock of Joseph's death quickly. During the week of mourning, she had many emotional outbursts, in which she wailed and screamed and sobbed for hours at a time. But it was a healing sorrow, and soon she began to look around her and see life as before. Basically a cheerful person, it wasn't long before she was showing her dimples again.

Then Rachel became pregnant.

It was too soon. Leah counted the days: only sixty days, two months, following the emotional shock of her beloved son's death. Leah wondered why God would give her a child now, after her devotion to the lifeless idols. Perhaps God had a reason.

The announcement of Rachel's pregnancy caused great rejoicing in the camp at Bethel. It snapped Jacob out of his melancholy, and his hearty laugh again resounded in the valley. Rachel's joy was reflected in the frequency with which she displayed her dimples. Her smiles and bright laughter endeared her to everyone in camp. Undoubtedly, she believed her teraphim, which she had trusted for so long, had finally fulfilled the promise of Joseph's name by giving her "Another."

Jacob immediately gave orders to move. They had been in Bethel five years, but he wanted his child to be born in Beersheba, which he considered his home. Rachel was four months into her pregnancy when the slow migration began.

Two months before Rachel's time of delivery, Leah insisted they stop. Rachel wasn't strong and wouldn't last until they reached Beersheba. Although Jacob was reluctant, he agreed because he trusted Leah's judgment.

They encamped near a small village called Ephrath, in Canaanite country. The countryside was hilly, and there was pasture, but Jacob asked his sons to continue on with the livestock toward Beersheba. Then he and his remaining family set up a semi-permanent camp at Ephrath.

Rachel was cheerful and optimistic. Leah insisted she spend most of her day in the tent, lying on cushions, sleeping as much as possible. Jacob agreed. When he spoke to her, she cheerfully obeyed, even though she insisted she would be all right, no matter what she did.

When at last Rachel's pains began, Leah set up a schedule for Bilhah, Zilpah, and herself to take turns at her bedside. It would be a long siege, and Leah knew the three women would need their strength near the end.

There was no rest for Rachel, however. After three days of unremitting pain, she was exhausted. Her screams had died away to moans, and Leah knew she couldn't endure much longer. Something would have to be done.

Leah knelt between Rachel's legs and explored the womb with her delicate fingers. It was as she feared: the baby was turned around so the feet instead of the head would come out first. Leah had had enough experience as a midwife to know that the mother seldom survived this kind of birth.

But she also knew that some of the pressure would be relieved if she could only turn the baby inside the womb. It was a delicate and dangerous process, something to be attempted only as a last resort. Leah was certain it had come to that.

Her sensitive fingers became her eyes, and slowly they began to work the baby around. Rachel's weak screams told Leah she was torturing Rachel. But it had to be done. The baby did move, ever so slowly, and finally Leah felt that the head was in the proper position. If the process of moving the child hadn't done too much damage, it should be an easier birth now, provided the child was born quickly.

Suddenly everything happened at once. Rachel's body tensed in a convulsive spasm. An unnatural flow squirted out on Leah's hands. Then the baby was there, fully born, a pulsing, living ejection from the tortured body of the mother.

Quickly Leah tied the cord, then cut it, and handed the baby to Bilhah. Bilhah had had enough experience to know what to do. She put the child on her knees, with its head lower than the body, and cleared the mouth. Then she gently jolted the baby until with a gasp the child began to cry.

"Be comforted, my lady," Bilhah called out to Rachel. "You have a healthy boy!"

Leah concentrated her attention on the problem of Rachel's desperate plight. Too much blood flowed from the womb, far more than was normal following a birth. Somehow she would have to stanch the flow of blood and fluid from the womb as quickly as possible.

She pressed cloth after cloth against the womb. She turned Rachel's body in different directions, sometimes crossing the legs. She elevated Rachel's buttocks, hoping the flow would cease if it had to move uphill. Nothing worked. Rachel's life was pouring out.

What should she do? Nothing in her experience or meager knowledge provided an answer to her desperate question.

Then the flow of blood and fluid began to slow. Rachel's body grew limp. Her breath came in short gasps. Leah felt for the pulse on her neck. It was terribly faint.

Rachel was dying.

What should she do? She looked around. Bilhah stood at the other end of the tent, gently cooing over the newborn baby. She would be no help. Nor Zilpah, wherever she was. There was nothing to be done. No way to stop it. Her sister would die. Soon.

She must tell Israel. He should be with his beloved wife at the end. It was his right.

She got to her feet and stumbled to the door of the tent. The early morning sunlight struck her face, contrasting with the darkness of the enclosed tent.

She paused a moment. Then she called, "Israel!"

"I'm here, Leah. How is she?"

Her husband had been nearby, then. Waiting. Leah became aware of her own disheveled condition. Her hands and robe were smeared with blood, and her face and hair felt gritty and streaked. Jacob's face reflected his horror as he looked at her.

"She's not well. Israel, she's dying. I'm sorry."

She spoke the words as gently as she could, but they struck Jacob as hard as if a tree had fallen on him. She heard him gasp and felt his hands tense as they gripped her shoulders. He started to go into the tent, but she stopped him.

"Israel, there are two things you must know. One is that you have a boy, a fine, healthy son. The other is that Rachel has placed the teraphim on either side of her bed with her."

"Teraphim?" His stunned mind groped for the meaning of her words. "Do you mean . . . Laban's teraphim? She has them?"

"She has always had them. I was afraid to take them away from her, because she seemed to need them. She felt that without them, she'd die."

"But they're idols, useless pieces of wood. They can't—"

"I know, Israel. But it would be unwise to take them from her now. Let them be until this is over. Now go to her, and be gentle. You may not have much time."

Leah stood just inside the doorway of the darkened tent and listened as Jacob went right to Rachel's side. With an effort he controlled his voice. "Rachel, my love. How are you?"

The question was absurd, but he was only half-thinking the words. Leah wondered if Rachel had already gone, but then she caught a whisper of a word from the bed.

" . . . knees. . . ."

Jacob gasped. Then he spoke urgently. "Give me the child!"

Bilhah obediently placed the child in his hands, and

Jacob then held the baby on Rachel's knees.

"Ben-oni!" she whispered.

Jacob's breath went out of his slowly. He turned to Leah. Leah knelt by Rachel's side and felt for the pulse in the throat. Her expert fingers found no sign of life.

"She's gone, Israel," she said gently.

"Leave us!"

Leah took the baby from Jacob, then rose and shepherded everyone from the tent. It was only right that Jacob and his beloved wife should be alone together in these first moments of death.

Nearly an hour later, Jacob emerged from the tent. By that time, Leah had washed herself and changed her robe.

"Leah! Where are you?" Jacob's voice was strong.

"I'm here, Israel." She hurried out of her tent and made her way toward the sound of his voice.

"Walk with me, please," he said.

She clutched his sleeve in the old familiar way and followed where he led. The sun was hot on her head, and she was grateful when he stopped in the shade of a large tree, somewhere in the unfamiliar Ephrath Valley.

They were alone. The family respected their need for privacy, and no one came near them. Bilhah and Zilpah would know what to do with Rachel's body.

"Leah."

"I'm here, Israel."

He didn't really want to talk. He wanted only to walk with her and share his sorrow. There evidently were no more tears left in him. He had spent them all inside the tent. He sought her hand on his sleeve and gripped it tightly.

She had no words to say to him, and instinctively she felt that any words she spoke now would be out of place and hollow. They stood together quietly. The only sound was the sighing of the breeze in the tree above. She was reminded of the Weeping Oak back in Bethel.

Finally, Jacob broke the silence.

"She wanted his name to be 'Ben-oni,' " he said.

Leah nodded. It was a horrible name. The meaning was plain: "Son of Sorrow." Appropriate enough, perhaps, but what a miserable name for a child to take through life with him. Names meant a great deal to them; it described the person and even predicted his lot in life. To begin life named "Son of Sorrow" meant to be sentenced to a lifetime of sorrow, not only in the eyes of others but in his own eyes as well. No child could live with that name and be happy.

"Will you call him that, Israel?"

"I don't know. It was her dying request. What do you think, Leah?"

She marshaled arguments against calling him by that horrible name. But she couldn't escape the bald statement Jacob had just uttered, that it was his beloved wife's dying request.

"Do what you think best, Israel." Leah could say no more. She sensed his disappointment in her answer, and she felt she had let him down. Always before, she had been ready with advice, with an opinion, with guidance. Now she was silent.

Some hidden instinct told her this must be Jacob's decision, and his alone. He would have to wrestle with God again. And all she could offer him was her understanding and the support of her presence.

17

The burial was held the same day, in the late afternoon. On the road to Ephrath, one of the servants had found a cave in the rocky hillside which would make an excellent tomb. Here Jacob brought the body that had meant so much to him in life. The entire family and many of the servants followed as he carried Rachel to the tomb.

Jacob entered alone, carrying Rachel to her final bed. Leah stood beside Zilpah and the others just outside, waiting for him. Bilhah held the newborn baby. It was a long wait. The silence of their vigil was not interrupted, not even by the rustle of wind in the trees.

"He's coming!" whispered Zilpah.

Leah heard a sound in the stillness. She knew Jacob stood at the entrance to the cave. Everyone waited for him to speak.

When he did, his voice was surprisingly strong and steady as he intoned the ritual words his family had used since the time of Abraham at burial ceremonies for family members: "God has given and God has taken away. Blessed be God!"

As Leah listened, she was reassured not only by the tone of his voice but by the words themselves. This was Israel speaking, not Jacob. His faith had won the struggle. If it hadn't, he might have stopped just short of the phrase "Blessed be God," thus bitterly accusing God of giving him his precious love, then brutally snatching her away. The final doxology showed that he accepted God's will, even if he didn't understand.

But Jacob wasn't finished. "Bring me the baby," he said.

Bilhah stepped forward instantly and handed the fully swathed baby into his hands. Jacob then tore off the cloth and held the baby naked before them all. "Behold Rachel's son!" he proclaimed loudly. "His name is Benjamin!"

Leah gasped. She knew what Jacob had done and guessed what it had cost him to disregard his wife's dying request. There must have been some agonized moments before he reached his decision. He was Israel—always the wrestler. The struggle had been between his need to honor the love he bore for his wife and his need to offer a child to God with an acceptable name. The child's need for an adequate name had won, but Leah marveled at the agony involved in reaching this decision.

Benjamin! An excellent name. The change from "Ben-oni" to "Benjamin," was small. But the change in meaning was great. "Son of My Right Hand." To place a child on his right hand meant that the child would be his favorite. The name changed from "Sorrow Boy" to "Favored Boy."

The favorite. Once again, Leah fought the familiar battle within herself. Only Rachel's sons were classified as the favorite. It wasn't fair! What about Reuben, the oldest, or Judah, who had shown leadership qualities? Why only Rachel's sons?

"Son of My Right Hand," of course, meant the inheritor of the Promise. The birthright. God's blessed one. It wasn't fair!

She lifted her eyes to the darkening skies, and in her mind echoed familiar words: *God, what about me? My sons? Can't you look on us with favor? Why must Rachel have it all?*

She thought she had left behind this struggle years ago. She had won a victory over herself. She had divested herself of every shred of jealousy for her sister and had accepted the way things were. But she knew she hadn't. It was still there, and she—like Israel—was wrestling with God.

Leah drew a deep breath. No. This couldn't go on. She must once again struggle with herself and win. She must overcome her petty jealousy. Put this in God's hands. God—not Leah—must bear the burden of deciding who the birthright child would be. God and God alone. And she would accept whatever that decision might be. Accept it cheerfully.

The child Benjamin would be hers to raise now. The heir of the Promise. And she would do her best, her cheerful best, to make him worthy of the blessing.

She had to. She could do nothing else.

"Leah."

Jacob stood before her, looking at her thoughtfully. She hadn't heard him approach. She had been so absorbed in her thoughts she hadn't been aware of the crowd milling around her. Her eyes! Was her struggle with herself made plain to her husband in her eyes?

"Walk with me, Leah." His voice was gentle. She grasped his sleeve as he led her down the path.

They were alone. She didn't know where they were, but the others had gone off and left them to their privacy. It didn't matter where they were, as long as she was with her husband. She sighed. Her whole life had been like that.

She had been holding his sleeve in the old familiar

way. Now he took her hand, and they stopped under a tree. Here in the shade it was even darker.

"Leah." His words were gentle. His eyes bored into hers. "Tell me what's troubling you."

She took a deep breath and tried to smile. "It's nothing, Israel. Just . . . sorrow. My sister. . . ."

"No. I don't think so. There's something else. What is it?"

The smile died on her lips and tears formed in her eyes. But she mustn't act like this. Her husband mustn't know of the deep struggle within her.

Jacob's next words caught her by surprise. "I think I know."

But how could he? She knew her expressive eyes gave away her secrets, but could he read in them this one? The depth and anguish of her own wrestling with God?

"All your life," Jacob continued, "you've been in a struggle with Rachel. You told me so, yourself. What was it, Leah? Jealousy?"

She nodded but could say nothing.

"Jealousy." Jacob spoke softly, tenderly. "You wanted my love. You accepted my God and gave me children, hoping for my love. And my love has gone to Rachel."

Again she nodded. Her eyes were staring at the ground. Jacob put his finger under her chin and tilted it, forcing her to look into his eyes.

"Don't you know you have my love? Not the same way I gave my love to Rachel, but it was love, nevertheless."

As she looked into his eyes, she realized what he said was true. Jacob's love was divided: To Rachel, he gave his body. To Leah, he gave his mind. But this wasn't a new thought; she had known this all along.

For years she had shared herself with him. She had walked at his side, always clutching his sleeve. She had challenged him, advised him, understood him. They were equals. But were they lovers?

Yes. In the most profound meaning of the word, they had found love. Two people were joined together in a union of companionship, of understanding, of . . . of *love*!

"Israel." She took a deep breath. "Our love is shared, at a very deep level."

"Yes." His arms went around her, and held her in a warm embrace. Into her ear he whispered, "And our love will help both of us face the future without Rachel."

For a moment they were silent. A breeze had sprung up, driving away the heat of the day. Dusk settled around them, and under the tree it turned dark.

Finally Jacob spoke. "Rachel's death," he said slowly, "was God's will."

Leah frowned. "God's will?" She leaned back slightly, and he released her from his embrace. "How do you know that?"

He looked down at her tenderly. "Do you remember the vow I made when we met Laban?"

"Yes. You promised never to cross the Mizpah boundary line. Why?"

"No. Not that vow. I made one earlier. Maybe you didn't hear it."

"Another vow? I don't recall anything about that."

Jacob sighed. "When Laban first told me that his teraphim were missing, I swore before the living God that whoever took those idols would die."

"Oh!"

Now Leah knew a part of her husband's struggle within himself. He had made the vow innocently, never suspecting that his beloved Rachel would be the victim of his sacred oath. Now, he believed, God had fulfilled the vow by taking Rachel's life.

"Israel, how can you be sure? You've told me many times, no one can be sure he knows the will of God."

Jacob paused. A frown creased his forehead. He pursed his lips.

"Yes." Again a pause. "You may be right. I *don't* know. When I was young, I was so sure of everything. Now. . . . I'm not sure of anything. Especially something so deep and mysterious as God's will!"

Leah stared into his face. "And if you think your vow might have led to Rachel's death, don't torture yourself. It's just too complicated to understand."

He nodded, returning her gaze. "You see things so clearly, Leah. Always, you've helped me. As you've helped me now."

"And you've helped me, my husband. More than you know."

He smiled. "Really? If so, then it's the first time!"

He took her hand and led her onto the road to start for their tents. The night had grown fully dark around them.

She squeezed his hand. "And Benjamin. . . ." She paused. " 'Child of My Right Hand.' Have no fears about him, Israel. I'll raise him and train him to be the heir of the Promise."

"*No!*"

The word erupted from his lips. She stopped and turned to him, surprised.

"What do you mean?"

"I mean he's not the birthright son!"

Leah gasped. "Israel, you don't mean that!"

"I do! I came to that decision as I stood at Rachel's tomb, mourning her death. He shall *not* receive the sacred blessing!"

"Why not?"

"Look what happened the last time I tried to impose my will on God's will! I selected Joseph, but he obviously wasn't God's choice."

"But then who *will* receive the birthright?"

"No one. Or rather, all eleven. Benjamin will be my favorite, yes. But he alone won't inherit the birthright—at least not from me."

"But I don't understand. Eleven men can't inherit the birthright." She paused, wrinkling her forehead. "Can they?"

"We'll find out." He laughed shortly, without humor. "I'm sick of making decisions I have no right to make in the first place. Let *God* choose the heir to the Promise!"

"Oh!"

They resumed their walk in the darkness. In silence. He would say no more and neither would she. All had been said.

Her husband was right. God *would* choose the heir to the Promise. He had said it earlier: no one can understand fully what is the will of God. So Israel would give the birthright blessing to all eleven of his sons.

But Benjamin would remain his favorite. One question remained: who would be God's chosen one?

Only God knew.

18

The family settled in Beersheba, where Jacob had lived as a child. Here Isaac and Rebekah, his parents, and Abraham and Sarah, his grandparents, had lived. The broad fertile plain supported Jacob's vast herds and flocks, and the seven wells which Abraham and Isaac had dug provided plenty of water.

The former inhabitants of the Beersheba plain scattered before the large, fierce clan which had invaded their territory. Perhaps they remembered the family from before, when Isaac and then Esau had ruled the land. When ten young men and their large numbers of herdsmen and livestock arrived, the Canaanites who lived there departed as fast as they could, leaving the area to Jacob.

As Benjamin grew to manhood, Jacob treated him as the favorite, keeping him home and teaching him to administer the business from their small city of tents on the Beersheba plain. Benjamin didn't flaunt his favoritism as Joseph had done. As a result, he was much loved and admired by his brothers.

Leah grew older and watched with interest her body's changes. She accepted them as the natural consequences of life. Her "drying-up time" had come. Now, she knew, she would be old and wrinkled. It didn't matter. Her life had been good to her. She was at peace.

Life *had* been good to her, she reflected. She had given her husband eight sons, including the two born to Zilpah, which were rightfully hers. She had mothered all twelve of Jacob's sons, training them in the ways of Jacob's God. She had managed the affairs of the large household, earning the love and respect of all the servants and herdsmen as well as the sons of Israel.

Best of all during those years was Jacob's love for her. It *was* love, she knew now, although a shared love. His physical and sexual love he had given to Rachel, visiting Leah's tent at night only to sire his sons. He had held her in his arms as a chore, a piece of work to be accomplished in the breeding of children. She smiled at this thought, accepting it. This was the way of men and beasts.

Nevertheless, she had his love. A strange kind of love, the kind Rachel never knew. Companionship. Sharing life with him had been delightful, especially in the fifteen years since Rachel's death. Jacob had sought her out repeatedly, spending many hours of every day with her. Their bond of understanding and affection had deepened. Call it love, she told herself. It wasn't romantic or erotic, but it *was* love.

The well used by the colony of Jacob's clan was a short walk from Leah's tent. Jacob appeared at the door of the tent every morning. Leah clutched his sleeve as they walked slowly toward the well. She tried to balance these walks between laughter and seriousness. They discussed the way Benjamin handled the accounts, or the birth of a new camel in the household herd, or purchases they would make from the next caravan bound for Egypt, or the latest foibles of their sons' wives and grandchildren. This was a happy time, a time to share their love.

One day, as they walked from the well, Leah

clutched her husband's sleeve in the old familiar way. Suddenly she felt a dull pain in her chest. She stumbled, leaning against her husband.

"Leah! What is it? What's wrong?" asked Jacob.

The pain in Leah's chest shot into her shoulder and spread down her left arm. She could feel a tenseness in her face and throat, a numbness in her lips. Her left foot was heavy.

"I don't know," she mumbled. "It's nothing. I'd like to lie down for a while."

She grasped Jacob's sleeve tightly, finding no strength in her hands. As she slumped against him, his arm went around her. Jacob shouted for help. Several of the servants ran to them, and they half carried, half dragged Leah to her tent.

The hours that followed were foggy to her. She heard Jacob giving urgent instructions, and Zilpah crying softly. She became vaguely aware of her sons crowding into the tent, kneeling by her bed, speaking to her. She couldn't reply.

And always Jacob stayed in the tent. He sat for hours by her bed, holding her hand, talking softly to her. She only half heard him, but the sound of his gentle voice was reassuring.

"Israel." She tried to say his name, but the word came out as a rattle in her throat. She had no control over her face, her jaws, her tongue.

Jacob bent closer to her, holding her hand. If she couldn't speak to him with words, perhaps her eyes could do her talking for her. He always knew what she was thinking just by looking into her eyes. She looked up at him, and was startled to see tears on his face.

"Leah," he said softly. Then in a rush of words, he added, "You shall be buried at Machpelah!"

She heard Zilpah's gasp, coming from behind Jacob.

157

To the servant, this was a totally thoughtless thing to say. He should have been encouraging her to live, talking soothingly about things they would be doing together in the future. Anything, except to speak of death.

But Jacob had spoken what was in his heart, and it meant much to her. They had never kept secrets from each other. Now they shared the final secret.

Jacob's words seared themselves deeply into Leah's mind. She couldn't control her facial muscles, but her eyes smiled at her husband. She knew exactly what he was saying.

Machpelah! The cave east of Mamre in Hebron was the family burial ground. Abraham had purchased the fields in which the caves were located many years ago, from Ephron the Hittite. Abraham and Sarah were buried there, as were Isaac and Rebekah. Everyone assumed that Jacob would be buried there some day.

His promise to bury her there meant far more than just providing a final resting place for her body. She would be there along with Sarah and Rebekah, the acknowledged matriarchs of the clan. It could only mean that Jacob considered *her* the matriarch, equal in status with Sarah and Rebekah.

She thought of Rachel, in her lonely tomb near Ephrath. She had always wondered why Jacob never brought her bones to Machpelah. Now she knew. Leah, not Rachel, was Jacob's matriarch, the mother of the clan.

Through the years of their marriage, she had always been "the other wife." Rachel was the beloved, the favorite. Leah had been married first, and she was the older sister, but she had accepted the subordinate role Jacob had apparently assigned her. She was the mother of Jacob's children, but Rachel had been the beloved wife.

Now Jacob was telling her something different. She thought of the years of companionship, when Jacob had spent his nights with Rachel and his days with Leah. She recalled those times of crisis when Jacob had always turned to her, not to Rachel, for help. In times of sorrow, Leah had consoled him. There was a bond between them far stronger than any bond between Jacob and Rachel.

Or was it stronger? No, not stronger. Different. He had loved Rachel with a physical, sexual love, that mystical attraction of the body when a man and woman came together as one. But the bond between Jacob and Leah was different. They had shared their minds and were one in spirit. Companionship. A deep sharing of themselves at life's most important level. That was the essence of their love.

In this tender moment of clarity, she opened her eyes and looked fully into his. No words were necessary, even if they were possible. What they saw in each other was far beyond what either of them could express in words.

She was at peace. And she closed her eyes forever.

A NOTE TO THE READER

This book was selected by the book division of the company that publishes *Guideposts*, a monthly magazine filled with true stories of people's adventures in faith.

If you have found inspiration in this book, we think you'll find monthly help and inspiration in the exciting stories that appear in our magazine.

Guideposts is not sold on the newsstand. It's available by subscription only. And subscribing is easy. All you have to do is write Guideposts, 39 Seminary Hill Road, Carmel, New York 10512. For those with special reading needs, *Guideposts* is published in Big Print, Braille, and Talking Magazine.

When you subscribe, each month you can count on receiving exciting new evidence of God's presence and His abiding love for His people.

Guideposts is also available on the Internet by accessing our homepage on the World Wide Web at http://www.guideposts.org. Send prayer requests to our Monday morning Prayer Fellowship. Read stories from recent issues of our magazines, *Guideposts*, *Angels on Earth*, *Guideposts for Kids* and *Positive Living*, and follow our popular book of daily devotionals, *Daily Guideposts*. Excerpts from some of our best-selling books are also available.